THE PSYCHIATRIST SAYS MURDER

THE PSYCHIATRIST SAYS MURDER

BY LUCY FREEMAN

ARBOR HOUSE
NEW YORK

To Sally
My Sister, My Friend

THE PSYCHIATRIST SAYS MURDER

ONE

He had the feeling of faint recognition. He thought he had seen her before but could not remember where.

The voice that made the appointment over the phone had sounded soft and seductive. The face and figure of the young woman now walking in the door matched the voice. Her slim shape was that of a model, her face that of a slightly cynical madonna. Glistening blond hair streamed straight below her shoulders. Shy gray eyes stared at him as though she were a schoolgirl; he, a stern principal.

"Please come in."

He led the way into the room with the green leather couch, the room in which, as one poetic patient put it, "the hidden secrets of the mind whirl off the four corners out into Central Park below."

Helene Garth looked nervously at the couch along the wall to the left. She whispered, "Do I lie on that?" as though to sink into its depths might be as devastating as stepping into quicksand.

"Why don't you sit here?"

He indicated a brown tweed armchair facing the

brown leather chair in which he sat, slightly to the rear of the couch. The two chairs were separated by a low teak table holding an oval glass ashtray and a box of Kleenex.

She sat down with a grimace, as if the chair were covered with small spikes. "You're very kind to see me." She coughed nervously.

"You said on the phone that you wanted to start treatment."

"That's what Dr. Winthrop, my doctor, advised. He called you, didn't he?"

"Yes. He's an old friend."

She was hanging on for dear life to the circular tortoiseshell handle of her black velvet purse. She wore black from head to toe: her short draped jersey dress, her mesh stockings, her platform patent-leather shoes, even her earrings, of black pearl. She looked as though she were in mourning. He wondered if someone close to her had died recently.

She said apologetically, "You're the first psychoanalyst I've seen outside the theater or films. You're different from what I expected."

"In what way?"

He was accustomed to patients telling him he was not their image of a psychoanalyst, but he wanted to know her thoughts.

"I expected a short man, rather bald, with a beard and bifocals. But you have no beard, you wear no glasses, and you're very handsome."

Then she said, as though she suddenly had to confess

it, "I had to force myself to come. I felt terrified as I stood outside your door. I wanted to run. But something made me press the bell."

"Over the phone you seemed pretty confident you wanted to start analysis."

"I do." The blond strands bobbed up and down in emphasis. "I'm desperate. I told Dr. Winthrop that. I asked his help because I didn't know where else to turn."

"Why do you feel desperate?"

She hesitated, then, "My husband hates me." She added, a whisper, "I think he wants to kill me."

No patient as yet had given *that* as a reason for going into analysis, he thought. Was it fantasy or the truth?

The first defiant tone entered that soft voice. "I'm *not* imagining things. My husband has told me several times he wishes I were dead. He says bitterly, 'Why don't you kill yourself and get us both out of this mess?' He can be very mean after a few drinks. He's used me like a punching bag. He's even knocked me to the floor when I dared answer back."

"Why do you stay with him?"

"We've been married only a year. I hate to admit defeat so soon. And——" she looked at Dr. Ames in embarrassment.

He waited, not wanting to rush her thoughts. He honored what he thought of as the rule of the three "p's"—never push a patient, never preach and never utter a platitude.

In a voice that was on the verge of tears she said, "It's

not easy to confess this but I also stay because there are times, though they have been few lately, when we do have sex. And it's the best I've ever had. I guess I still love my husband in a strange way, in spite of his cruelty."

"What does he think of your starting analysis?"

"He wants me to try anything that might straighten me out, he says." And, defensively, "I'll use my own money to pay for it."

"Do you work?"

"I did before we were married. I was featured as a dancer in *Leading Lady*. Under my maiden name—Helene Benson."

That was where he had seen her. She had appeared as a striptease dancer in an exciting specialty number in a hit Broadway musical. The audience had applauded wildly at the end, wanting more of her graceful, sensuous dancing.

"What does your husband do?"

"He's a stockbroker on Wall Street. He works very hard. Even weekends, when he studies financial newspapers and magazines. Our honeymoon was his first vacation in years. We took a Caribbean cruise. Nine ports in two weeks."

She drifted off into reverie. He asked, "What are you thinking?"

"I was remembering moments that were happy." Sadly, "Though others were not so pleasant."

He waited, heard her sigh.

She said, "The first few nights, after dinner and a few

dances, he couldn't wait to make love. I thought I was the luckiest woman in the world."

She stopped and looked at Dr. Ames, very upset. Then, "I think it was about the seventh night, he seemed drunker than usual. Instead of making love he started to curse me. He called me a cheat and a whore. He said I had deceived him. Suddenly he raised his fist and struck me hard across the face. I reeled and fell to the floor.

" 'Get out, you bitch!' he yelled at me. 'Go away and leave me alone.'

"Lying there on the floor, stunned, I wondered what I should do. You can't go far on a ship. But he soon fell in a stupor on his bed. When I heard him snore, I dragged myself up off the floor and crept into my bed. I moved cautiously. I didn't want to wake him and get beaten again. Then I cried for hours. I couldn't imagine what I had done to make him hate me so.

"In the morning he apologized. He said he had been so drunk he didn't even know what he did or said but thought somehow he had hurt me. He kissed me passionately. We made love. And the rest of the trip he was as charming as he could be, as if to make it up to me.

"After we got back to New York, about two weeks later the same thing happened again. And again he apologized. And again we made love. And again I forgave him. Another two weeks passed. Then the same thing again. But this time he didn't want to make love. He was angry when he woke in the morning. He didn't speak to me for a week. And it's grown worse an !

worse. Last week he snarled at me, 'Why don't you kill yourself and get us out of this mess?' "

Dr. Ames said, "Tell me about your life before you were married."

She smiled faintly, her first smile since entering the office. "That covers a lot of experiences during my twenty-nine years in New York."

"Were you born in the city?"

"And never left it. I got an undergraduate degree in psychology at Barnard. Then I studied modern dance. More than anything else in life, I wanted to be a dancer. Ever since my mother enrolled me in ballet school as a child. My father didn't want me to go on the stage. He thought it was a really disreputable life. But after he died, two years ago, I tried out for a part in *Leading Lady*. I got it."

All this was said in her soft, almost breathless voice, the same voice in which she had spoken her few lines in the show. He thought of the contrast between her sweet, shy manner and the sense of abandon and sensuality of her movements onstage. It took an artist with great control to arouse an audience as she did.

"Did you give up dancing after you married?" he asked.

"Gladly. It wasn't long before I realized my father was right. I soon had it with the so-called glamorous life of the theater. The backbreaking work. And the backbiting behind the scenes. Too much!"

She added earnestly, "I do want to make a success of my marriage. And I want to start analysis with you so I

16

can make the marriage work. I have some awareness of what psychoanalysis can do. That's why I could accept Dr. Winthrop's advice and call you. Otherwise I would have been too scared."

"Do you have relatives in New York?"

"My mother and brother live here. My mother has lived alone since my father died of a heart attack. My father owned five factories that made plastics goods. He left us a fairly large inheritance from their sale after his death."

"What does your brother do?"

"He's an artist. He studied in Paris for three years."

"Is he married?"

"Divorced. After five years of a marriage that didn't work. There were no children. His wife married another man right after they split."

Dr. Ames looked at the clock across the room and said quietly, "The time is up. But could you come back Thursday at two?"

"Yes, of course."

She looked at him as though he had just plunged into a stormy sea to rescue her. There were tears in her eyes.

She stood up, said, "Do excuse my tears. This is the first time in years that anyone has been truly kind to me."

"Don't apologize for tears," he said. "If you feel like crying, please cry."

"Thank you for understanding," she said, voice low.

And shot out of the room as though a gun had gone off to signal the start of a fifty yard dash.

TWO

"Do I lie down this time?"

The soft voice quavered, the gray eyes seemed to plead with him to save her from her fate, whatever it might be. Did she fear death, rape? What was her fantasy? He would never give an interpretation so early in an analysis.

She wasn't wearing black today, but a dark-blue satin pants suit, a string of white pearls that dangled below her breasts and a cluster of smaller pearls as earrings. She might have stepped from the pages of the *Vogue* that lay on the mahogany table in his reception room.

"Whatever you wish." He wanted her to set her own psychic pace.

"I think I'll still sit, if you don't mind."

She perched uncertainly on the brown tweed chair. "Where do I start?"

"Just say whatever comes to mind."

These words were uttered not as command but with the conviction that whatever her thoughts, they would bear psychic fruit. There was no right or wrong about thoughts in an analyst's office.

She was silent a moment. Then, "When I got home

after seeing you Tuesday, Al demanded that I tell him what happened here. I didn't think I should talk about it. Isn't that right?"

"It doesn't matter. Your husband was probably very curious."

"He said he hoped the analysis would help me but doubted it. He said I was beyond help. I asked why. He said I wasn't a 'woman.' He accused me again of cheating him. What does he mean?"

"We don't know," said Dr. Ames. "We can't see into his mind."

But he thought, when a man feels a woman has cheated him, unconsciously he means she has failed to present him with a penis. Little boys imagine their mother possesses a penis, just like their father. When they find out she does not, they have the fantasy she has been mutilated and they may suffer the same fate if they are "bad." Albert Garth, an emotionally immature man, who had to rely on his fists, not his penis, imagined that a lovely, sexy young woman like Helene Benson would make him potent. When she could not—no woman could—he felt enraged and accused her of cheating him. The homosexual carries the fantasy of the phallic woman one step further. He refuses to have sex with any creature who does not possess a penis, so frightened is he of what he imagines is the castrated feminine form.

Helene Garth was saying, "Al was drunk last night, as usual. I don't understand how he gets through the day.

Except that he takes a pill in the morning. Alcohol at night to put him to sleep and a pill to wake him up."

"So he never has to face what he really feels," commented Dr. Ames.

"The only time he doesn't drink is when his daughter visits. He's ashamed to let her hear him spitting insults at me."

"Where does she live?"

"Amy's a freshman at Vassar. During vacation she stays with her mother. Al says he divorced his first wife, Marietta, because she deceived him. For years she wouldn't even talk to him, because she hated him so much, he says."

"Do you hate him?"

She looked troubled. "I don't know." She paused. "I hate him when he drinks and hits me. But then the next morning, when he looks so ashamed, I feel sorry for him. He can be enormously charming when he's sober. And, as I told you, once in a while we have sex. And then all the misery seems unimportant."

She mused, "Sometimes, after he's been drinking he falls asleep, and I creep into bed and snuggle close. Just to feel the warmth of his body is a comfort to me."

"You pay a high price for that comfort. You could share the same closeness with a man who treated you with respect. Who loved you."

"I think Al loves me. As much as he can love anybody." She sighed, then said, "He never denies me money. I have all the dresses and jewelry and fur coats I need. We live lavishly." And triumphantly she stated, "He's left me a million dollars in his will."

"But not out of love."

"Out of what, then?" She looked puzzled.

"Out of guilt. It's hardly show of love for a man to treat a woman like a punching bag. Or ask her to kill herself to get him out of a 'mess.' "

Defensively, "That's only when he's drunk."

"It's then he can tell you how he really feels. It's easier for him to keep up pretenses when he's sober."

"That isn't too often, I admit. You know, Dr. Ames, I pray each day for the market to go up. He's the cruelest when it goes down because it's then he drinks the most. As though I'm responsible for the loss of money."

"He holds you responsible in his unconscious for the loss of many things. Your husband may be a dangerous man when his fantasies let him place the blame on you."

For the first time she looked at him in alarm. "Do you think I'm really in danger?"

"I don't know how seriously disturbed your husband is. But I wouldn't take his threats lightly. I would ask myself, if I were you, why you stay with him."

"For the moments that are good."

"Don't you trust yourself to find another man who will give you many more pleasurable moments without the need to beat you?"

"Why do I take the beatings, Dr. Ames?"

"A good question."

"Please tell me why," she begged.

He was reluctant to answer. It would be intellectual exercise, not analysis. But he sensed she was desperate for the slightest clue to help her understand why she stayed with such a sadistic man.

"I would hazard a guess that when you were a little girl your father was cruel to you at times but at other times was very seductive and affectionate. This formed your concept of 'man.' You later sought the same see-sawing between punishment and forgiveness in a husband. You have not been able to accept a man who would *not* treat you with contempt and brutality one moment and bestow on you a kind of grudging affection the next."

She lowered her eyes, sudden tears in them. She asked, in a muffled voice, "You think so little of me, Dr. Ames?"

"Do you think so little of yourself?" he asked.

As though diving into the midst of her thoughts she said abruptly, "I was so embarrassed when she told me she felt sorry for me. She said she hated to see her father treat me so terribly."

"Amy?"

"Yes."

"Do you like her?"

"She's very sweet. Defenseless. Not at all like her father. Or her mother, who is a sort of fashion-plate virago."

"What made Amy say she thought her father treated you terribly?"

"One night when she came for supper, Al lost his temper because dinner was late. We had just hired a new cook and she didn't serve on time. Al carried on like a madman."

"What did he say?"

"He called me an incompetent cunt who couldn't even manage an apartment with all the money in the world available. He said I was good only to walk the streets. That I should have been a hooker. He must have had a few drinks even though he knew Amy was coming."

"Does Amy know that he beats you up?"

"I've never mentioned her father's behavior to her."

"Fathers are sacred, aren't they?"

"What do you mean?" She looked very upset.

"Tell me something about your father, Mrs. Garth."

"I adored him." She spoke with deep conviction. "And he adored me. When my brother was born—Evan is two years younger than I—my mother loved him best. But I didn't care. I knew my father loved me best. And when he died, I wanted to die too. I remember thinking, 'Who will care about me now?' "

"You and your father were very close."

"Very." Tears came to her eyes. "I can't even talk about him without crying." She paused. Then, "Though I remember one time I hated him passionately."

"When was that?"

"I was about eight years old. I wanted to buy a box of chocolates, and I took some money from my mother's purse without asking her. She always had given me permission to do this when I did ask. She told my father I 'stole' the money. He whipped me and sent me to my room without supper. I remember lying on the bed promising myself to get even with both of them when I grew up. Then Evan, my dear brother, crept upstairs to comfort me. He came into the room, put his arms around me, kissed me and pulled a little package of food out of his pocket. I have always loved Evan. Once or twice, after Al beat me up, I ran over to my brother's studio apartment to spend the rest of the night on his sofa."

Dr. Ames noted that he had not been wrong about her father's lack of tenderness. He asked, "Did your father ever strike your brother?"

"Once he whipped Evan, much more severely. I can still hear Evan crying out in pain."

"How old was he?"

"About ten."

"Do you recall the reason for the whipping?"

She hesitated, then, "The mother of the little boy next door, Evan's best friend, called up my mother. She said she had caught the two boys naked and touching each other's penises. All hell broke loose when my father got home that night and mother told him what had happened. My father was very upset, he said the whole family was disgraced, and he took Evan into his bedroom and hit him with his leather belt. I loved my father, but God, would you believe a parent would do such a thing in this day and age?"

"Depends on the parent."

"It's a wonder Evan was even able to marry, isn't it? If he was punished so young and made to feel sex was bad?"

"Never underestimate the strength of the sexual drive. It often overpowers even the toughest of childhood traumas."

Then he said, "The time is up. I could see you next Monday at two, if that's convenient."

"Not until then?"

Her voice was panicky, as though she felt something dangerous might happen before Monday.

"Starting next week, I could see you four times a week at two o'clock, Monday through Thursday."

"I'm very grateful for your giving me that much time." Adding, in the little girl voice, "Do you really think you can help me, Dr. Ames?"

"I think we can work together," he said.

As she walked out of the room, this time more slowly, he thought, in spite of your inability to get away from a man who beats you and tells you he wishes you would kill yourself.

THREE

"A difficult day?"

This was not Mary's usual greeting and he wondered what sign of anxiety she saw on his face as he entered the apartment. He lived only a short drive from his office through the park, now sheathed in early summer green.

"The usual. Except for the new patient. I saw her for the second time today. A young woman sent by old Doc Winthrop. He thought she might be suitable for analysis."

Not everyone was. You needed a certain amount of what Freud called "ego strength" to bear the psychic pain that was an inevitable part of psychoanalysis, as defenses slowly fell and the tabooed desires of childhood emerged.

" 'Happy are they who can hear their detractions and put them to mending.' " Mary's voice was playful. "Who said that?"

"Shakespeare."

"Which play?"

"*Much Ado.*"

She gasped. "How did you know? You're not a

Shakespearean scholar. I watched Papp's production on television last night while you were teaching, and memorized the line. It seemed so applicable to your work."

"You don't know everything about my past, dear lady. Shakespeare helped me decide to become a psychoanalyst. After acting in a few of his plays in college, I decided I wanted to work at analyzing the vagaries of human emotions."

"Do you think your new patient can put her detractions to mending?"

"I hope I can help her to."

As though to dismiss thoughts of the office he announced, "I'm stark-raving starved. What's for dinner?"

"Steak. Rare. I've finally trained Carrie to snatch it off the broiler before it resembles brown leather, though it kills her to do so. She thinks we're savages to eat meat that raw."

The word "kill" brought to mind Helene Garth's fear: "I think he wants to kill me."

Was this a projection of her own secret wish to kill a man who struck her, a man of whom she was obviously terrified but from whom she could not escape? Or was it a reality? Did her husband wish to kill her because in some way she threatened him? Did she really need the police more than an analyst? But he decided he'd thought enough about his patients for that night.

"Where's my drink?" he demanded.

Before dinner Mary and he usually enjoyed one or

two drinks in front of their fireplace. Even in spring and summer, they loved sitting there.

"Coming right up, oh tyrannical one."

"You don't know what a tyrant is." He thought of Helene Garth's husband.

"I consider you a well-analyzed tyrant."

In ironic tone, he said, "Thank you very much." Then, as she handed him a scotch and water, he asked, "Heard from Carol?" Their nineteen-year-old daughter was in her second year at Bennington.

"She wrote that she plans to spend summer vacation touring France with three classmates." She paused. Then softly, "Remember our honeymoon in Paris?"

"Every second of it."

As he cut into steak so rare it ran blood, he noticed Mary was wearing a pale-blue dinner dress. "You look lovely tonight," he said. "Is that new?"

"Wore it in Paris on our honeymoon."

"You can't mean it." He put his fork down in surprise.

"Just wanted to see if you remembered what I did wear."

"To be honest, I don't. What *were* you wearing?"

She blushed. "Nothing, most of the time."

He raised high a glass of Chablis. Mary served white wine with both red meat and fish, claiming she made her own rules about alcohol at the dinner table.

"Here's to memories of a happy honeymoon," he said.

"Aren't all honeymoons happy?" she asked.

29

"Not all."

He thought of another honeymoon, one he had heard Helene Garth describe, a honeymoon of hate rather than love, the bride struck savagely to the floor by an enraged husband. He heard once again the soft voice asking, "Do you think I'm really in danger?"

He had warned her she might be. He wondered if he had been too casual in his warning. He could not tell her what to do, for that was not analysis. But, he thought, he might have made clearer some of the risks of remaining with such a brutal man.

Here he was, thinking again of a patient. There must be something about her that haunted him, something he could not as yet put his finger on.

FOUR

The following Monday, Helene Garth was late for her third session. It was seven minutes past the start of her hour when Dr. Ames heard the outer door to the reception room open and close.

He went to the reception room to ask her to enter. Her body was slumped in a chair as though she never wanted to get out of it. The face that turned to his was pale, the usually expressive eyes were blank, and the blond hair, carefully combed for her previous sessions, was a mop of tangles. Even her brown silk dress looked as if she had thrown it on hurriedly.

"Please come in," he said.

She walked in like a zombie. As she sat down in the brown tweed chair, she looked at him dumbly.

"What's the matter?" There was concern in his voice.

"You were right," she said tonelessly. "He is dangerous. He tried to kill me."

"Tell me what happened."

"I wouldn't have believed it! It's the most frightening feeling in the world to realize someone is trying to kill you." Her body seemed to shrivel in fear.

He waited for her to go on, for the feeling of terror to subside.

"Saturday night we went to a party given by some friends. Naturally, Al drank more than he should. When we got back to the apartment, he called me 'slut' and 'bitch,' as usual. As he raised his fist to hit me, I ran out on the terrace. We have an eight-room penthouse on the thirty-fifth floor, with a terrace bordering the south and west sides.

"Al followed me. He's a tall man, powerfully built. And a handsome man. Women fall all over him. They find him fascinating, as they did at the party that night.

"He stumbled over to where I was cowering in a corner. He said, 'I'm going to kill you—right now.'

"I pleaded, 'Please, Al. You've had too much to drink.'

" 'Right this minute,' he said.

" 'I'll leave in the morning, if that's what you want,' I said. 'I don't want to stay here if you feel this way.'

" 'You won't leave me,' he said. 'No woman walks out on me.'

"He made a grab for my throat. I managed to squirm away. I started to scream. I screamed and I screamed. The maid heard me and came running from her room, off the kitchen. When Al saw her, he let me go. He stalked off to the bedroom.

" 'Thank you, Vera,' I said, knowing she had probably saved my life. For the first time, I really felt he wanted to kill me."

"Then what did you do?" He wondered if this had been enough to convince her to leave.

"I couldn't stay in that apartment. I didn't want to

disturb Evan at that hour. I thought of the nearest hotel, the Carlyle. I fled without even a nightgown. I didn't want to go into the bedroom—I thought he might attack me again.

"I took an empty suitcase from the hall closet and caught a taxi to the Carlyle, which luckily had a vacant room."

"And the next day?"

"I phoned Al. In a way, I guess, I didn't want to believe what had happened. He was, as I knew he would be, very apologetic. He said he had called my mother and my brother, trying to find me. He begged me to come back. He promised he would never touch another drop of alcohol."

She fell silent.

"And?"

"I went back to pack some clothes and leave forever. But he wouldn't let me go. He threw his arms around me, kissed me ardently, said he would never touch me again except in love. We—we—" She stopped.

"Made love?"

"Yes. And it was out of this world. Incredible, how there can be so much rage one moment, so much passion the next. And that night Al couldn't have been more considerate. He didn't have a drink. Even so, I told him that I intended to leave. He asked me to talk it over with you before making up my mind. I said I would— odd, isn't it? Suddenly he uses you as an ally after telling me you can't do me any good."

"You still look pretty shaken."

"I am. I thought I was under control before coming here. But once I walked in the door of your reception room I started reliving Saturday night. What do you think I should do?"

"I think you should take a long look at the situation you have placed yourself in and at its dangers."

"You think it's dangerous, don't you?"

"Consider what you've just told me. Your husband tried to choke you to death on the terrace. If he had succeeded, he might have thrown your body down to the street and claimed it was suicide. Or an accident."

There was alarm on her face. "I really have no choice, do I? I must leave."

"I would think that's the wise thing to do."

"But Al said no woman would ever leave him. He might come after me and kill me."

"I think your chances of staying alive are greater the more distance you put between yourself and this man. And there's always the police."

This was the closest he had ever come to advising a patient to take a specific action. But Helene Garth, he felt, was trapped in a highly explosive situation. No one would diagnose her as psychotic, for she was not violent, she was not irrational, she was outwardly a beautiful, reasonable woman who only wanted love from her husband. But as the victim of violence she unconsciously sought, she needed advice, and, he believed, in this instance he was justified in suggesting she leave her husband in order to save her life.

"Do you think I should get out tonight?" she asked.

"I think it would be best if you leave before he gets home. Otherwise you'll either face an argument or, if he's drinking again, face his rage."

"Thank you." Relief in her voice, her eyes. "You give me the courage to go through with this." Then she asked, "Will you still see me?"

"Perhaps the question is rather, will you still see me? You gave as your reason for coming here that you wanted to hold your marriage together."

She said earnestly, "I realize now that is impossible. And also that I need your help if I am to change my life. I want to find out what drove me to marry such a cruel man."

The first step in understanding the self, he thought, is being able to ask, "Why did I do that?" instead of, "Why did this happen to me?"

"Weren't your mother and brother worried when your husband called trying to find you?" Dr. Ames asked.

"I phoned each of them right away and told them I was okay."

"Did you explain why you were at the Carlyle?"

She hesitated, then, "I didn't have to. They know Al drinks a lot, gets brutal, and I have had to leave the apartment before at times."

"What was their reaction?"

"My mother keeps insisting I leave Al at once. My brother says if I stay, I have to make sure Al doesn't drink."

"Not a very realistic approach."

"I know that. But my brother remained in a miserable marriage for years before he finally could break it up. He thinks marriage is sacred."

"Your mother and father never separated. It may have been difficult for him to do so."

"And difficult for me too, Dr. Ames?" A sweet-voiced question.

"Yes."

"But I *am* going to leave Al. I'm going home and pack my clothes and books. I've never felt that apartment belonged to me in any way, anyhow. I wander around it like a lost stranger. I feel I'm allowed to live there only because Al lets me."

That was the way a little girl feels about the house in which she grows up, he thought. She is not the mistress, her mother is, and she lives there only because of her father's kindness. When Helene Garth's father died—the man she adored—she unconsciously threw herself into a marriage with an angry man. When he threatened to kill her, it gratified her unconscious wish to rejoin her father in death. Had she not told Ames that, when her father died, she wished she were dead, too, and she saw no reason to go on living? By marrying a man who threatened to kill her, she was carrying out this wish.

"If you leave him, your husband may cut you off without a cent," Dr. Ames said. "But that's better than being dead and unable to collect a penny."

"Do you think that's the reason he wants to kill me?" She looked alarmed.

"It may be one of many. There are usually many unconscious reasons that drive a man to kill."

She said proudly, "I have money enough from my father's estate to live without Al's support."

"You could also go back to work, if you needed, couldn't you?"

"Yes. If I needed to," she said half-heartedly.

As she left she told him, "I'll see you tomorrow at two. I don't know where I'll be living. But I know I'll be here at that hour."

There seemed to be new strength in her soft voice.

FIVE

The next day at 1 PM, between patients, he picked up the phone to ask the service if there were any messages. The service announced, with no surprise, as though it were a regular occurence, "Lieutenant Jack Lonegan of the 19th Precinct called. He asked if you would call him back as soon as you were free." She gave the number.

Dr. Ames smiled as he dialed the number. He thought of Lonegan with warm feelings. The year before he had helped Lonegan, then a detective first class, to solve the murder of Jonathan Thomas, a patient of his. Why was Lonegan calling him now? Had another patient been murdered? Ridiculous. No analyst in the world would come up against such odds—two patients murdered within a year. If it were true, who would come to him to be analyzed, he asked himself wryly. Then answered himself, "Suicides."

"Lieutenant Lonegan, please," he said to the policeman who answered. "Dr. William Ames calling back."

Then he heard Lonegan's deep, friendly voice with its Irish brogue and cynical humor. "How are you, Doc? It's been a long time. I thought we were going to get together now and then for a drink."

"I was waiting for you to call. You're the busy one, judging by crime statistics. So, you're a Lieutenant now. Congratulations."

"Yeah! Thanks to you. If you hadn't caught the Thomas killer, there wouldn't have been a promotion. I owe you one for that, Doc."

"You don't owe me anything. It meant a lot to me to help you find his murderer."

There was a pause on the other end of the wire. Then Lonegan said, "Doc, I need your help again. There's been a murder in my precinct in which a patient of yours is involved."

My God, Dr. Ames thought, I wasn't able to help her in time. Garth carried out his threat.

He said grimly, "Tell me the details, Lonegan. When did he do it?"

"When did he do what, Doc?" Puzzled voice.

"When did Albert Garth kill his wife?"

"You on junk, Doc?" the Lieutenant asked jokingly.

"You know me better than that. Once in a while one too many scotches, maybe. But a drug addict I'm not."

"Well here's the facts and see what *you'd* think if anyone came out with that crack. Garth didn't murder anyone. You got the name right but not the gender of the corpse. The body we found belonged to a man. Albert Garth was the one who got killed."

"Garth is dead?" Dr. Ames could hardly believe it. How ironic. Both he and Helene Garth had been afraid she would be murdered by her husband. Instead, *he* turned out to be the victim.

"The body was found about eight this morning by Mrs. Garth and the cook. He'd been stabbed three in the chest. There were no fingerprints in the room other than the family's and the cook's. Mrs. Garth said she did not see her husband last night—that he wasn't home when she went to bed about midnight and she didn't hear a thing after that."

Then he asked, "Will you help me on this case, Doc?"

Dr. Ames was proud he had been able to pinpoint the murderer of the publisher Jonathan Thomas. But he was trained to help the emotionally troubled discover and come to terms with inner conflicts. He was content to leave the solving of murder to the tax-paid sleuths who worked New York's streets of violence.

He didn't want to offend Lonegan, but he didn't really want the job. He said, "I enjoyed working with you on the Thomas case. And I'm honored that you want to work with me again. But I'm not the detective—you are."

"You're a sort of detective, Doc. You get into corners of the mind I can't reach. Corners I don't even know exist."

"Thanks, Lieutenant. That's well put." He knew Lonegan really meant it. He was cynical, but he was sincere.

"This case is harder to crack than the Thomas one. We don't have the weapon. *Nobody's* alibi stands up. I need you." He added, half a joke, "Maybe this time you'll help make me Captain."

"By the way, how did you happen to know my

connection to Mrs. Garth?" He did not want to reveal that she was a patient unless she had done so first.

"She told me you were her shrink."

"Did you tell her you knew me?"

"No. I protected you, Doc."

Dr. Ames chuckled. "Thanks. It's been quite a while since anyone protected me."

"And I'm asking you to protect me, Doc. Help me out, anyway."

"You mean interview the suspects?"

"You sure learned the jargon. That's just what I mean."

"Who are the suspects, Lonegan?"

"Don't needle me, Doc. You know them better than I do. That gorgeous Mrs. Garth must have told you lots about her life that she didn't spill to me in two hours of questioning in that blood-soaked room."

"Aren't you exaggerating about the blood?" He couldn't help asking; it was Mary's influence—Mary and her avid reading of murder mysteries. She would have wanted to know all the details.

"He was a big guy and he bled like a stuffed pig. The blood ran all over their white carpet. You might say wall-to-wall blood."

"What killed him?"

"Some sort of small but very sharp knife."

"No idea who did it?"

"None. We're totally lost."

"Go over the suspects for me."

"Helene Garth, his second wife. Marietta Garth, his

first wife. His daughter, Amy, by the first wife. Helene Garth's mother, Mrs. Annette Benson. Helene Garth's brother, Evan Benson. Plus maybe an enemy or two in the financial world who wanted revenge for a lousy tip on the market."

"That's all?"

"One more. I forgot Helene Garth's boyfriend."

"Boyfriend?"

In spite of his professional calm, based on the belief that nothing any human being said, thought, or did, including murder and the most perverse of sexual acts, could upset his emotional equilibrium, Dr. Ames was surprised. Helene Garth had not mentioned a man in her life other than her husband.

"That actor friend of hers. Wait a minute. I'll find his name in my notes."

Dr. Ames heard the sound of Lonegan shuffling paper. "Noel Marvin. He was in her last show. I understand it was a hit."

"I saw it. Helene Garth did a great dance number. And I remember Noel Marvin. He was very convincing as the second male lead. He played the young director of an avant-garde film. Sort of a likable, comic character."

"Likable, comic characters commit murder regularly," said Lonegan bitterly. "And his alibi holds up about as well as the rest of them."

"How did you check the alibis so quickly?" Dr. Ames was impressed.

"The two detectives working under me are whizzes.

They've been out checking since nine this morning. They learned that the daughter, Amy, did not spend the night in her room at college as she said she did. That the first wife walked by herself for hours in Washington Square but no one saw her. That Noel Marvin walked all the way from rehearsal on Broadway to his apartment in Greenwich Village but no one saw *him*. That Helene Garth was in her apartment waiting for her husband to come home from a meeting, according to the cook, who went into her room at eight o'clock and couldn't prove that Mrs. Garth didn't slip out later. That her brother, an artist, felt inspired and spent the evening painting in his apartment so no one saw *him*. That their mother, Mrs. Benson, was watching television alone in her apartment so no one saw *her*."

"Looks like you've got work on your hands, Lonegan."

"I've got to depend on you for the psychological approach, Doc. Any one of them could have killed Garth and could have wanted to. They all had a motive. Be a sport. Help me out."

Dr. Ames sighed. "Lonegan, I like and respect you. But I don't have the time to be a psychoanalyst *and* a detective."

"Not even if it involves the life of your pretty patient?"

"What do you mean?" What did Lonegan know that he had not revealed?

"There's no proof, Doc, that she didn't murder him."

"Do you have any proof she did?"

44

"Not so far. But she's just as much a suspect as anyone else. And you know what, Doc?"

"What Lonegan?"

"I think she has the strongest motive of anyone."

"Which is?"

"Money. Garth set up a trust fund for his daughter when he was divorced, so she doesn't have that motive. He paid his first wife alimony which lasts until she remarries and which continues out of a special fund in case of his death, so *she* doesn't have the motive of money either. But your patient gets money only in case of his death. A cool million or so."

"Money isn't everything," he said lamely. The beatings Helene Garth had taken, Dr. Ames thought, were an even stronger motive.

"In the case of murder, it often figures big, Doc. I'm asking for the last time. Will you *please* give a hand? Strictly speaking, a head?"

In spite of the small inner voice that cautioned him against it, Dr. Ames felt an urge for adventure, rebellion against sitting in one chair, hour after hour, day after day, year after year. Though his job was, in large part, to help the individual better protect himself by understanding his own self-destructive impulses, why should he not occasionally help bring to justice someone who had committed murder, thus protecting society?

He said to Lonegan, "Before I make my decision, I'd have to talk to Mrs. Garth. Because she's a patient, I need her approval."

"When do you see her next?"

"She was supposed to be here today at two. But under the circumstances, I certainly don't expect her to show up. I'm assuming she'll come tomorrow, though."

"If she does, will you ask her if she has any objection to your working on the case?"

"Sure, I will." That far he would commit himself.

"I'll call you about four tomorrow to see what she says."

After he hung up, Dr. Ames wondered why Helene Garth had not mentioned her involvement with Noel Marvin. Perhaps Lonegan was jumping to the wrong conclusion, perhaps it was not an affair but a friendship with no conflicts really distressing for her. Or, perhaps, she did not as yet trust her analyst enough—after all, she had only seen him three times—to confess what she believed might detract from a favorable image of herself. A husband who beat her might be acceptable, but not an adulterous relationship.

He called back the service to find out if she had phoned to cancel her hour. He doubted she would show up, much as she needed the solace and help she felt from him. He recalled she had told him he was the first person in years to show her kindness.

"Any further messages?" he asked the service.

"Mrs. Garth just called. She said to tell you she couldn't get here today but would be here tomorrow at her regular hour. She said you probably would know why."

"Thank you."

He knew why, and the world would know as soon as

the evening newspapers hit the street and the nightly news programs hit the air. The murder of a millionaire stockbroker in his East Side penthouse was prime-time news and a front-page headline.

He felt sorrow for Helene Garth, who must have been suffering deeply because of hidden death wishes for the murdered man and her guilt over them.

He wondered if she had any idea who had murdered her husband. Or if she was just as much in the dark as Lonegan. A man with the temperament of Garth would have enemies: violence begets violence. Perhaps an unknown enemy had killed him and accidently saved Helene Garth's life—a life she seemed unable to save by herself. She had not packed and left the apartment as she had said she intended to do. Was it just her lack of emotional strength, he wondered, or had something changed her mind?

SIX

Mary met him at the door, drink in hand for him. He kissed her lightly, then gulped the first few swallows of scotch almost greedily.

"I needed that, as they say."

She looked at him, silent, waiting for explanation, as he did with his patients, and he laughed, knowing how contagious responses were when people felt close.

"You wouldn't believe this, Mary," he said, leading the way into the living room and throwing himself on the sofa. "I got a call today from Jack Lonegan asking me to help him solve another murder. Remember him?"

"Your good friend," she said. "How could I forget?"

"Well I seem to be his at the moment."

"Who's been murdered this time?" Facetiously, she added, "Another of your patients?"

"Mary, Mary!" In reproof. "Isn't one murdered patient enough for a lifetime?"

"Sorry. Then who?"

"Well—er—" He discovered he felt on the defensive.

Again she waited in silence.

He sighed. "This time it happened to be the husband of one of my patients."

"Oh, no!" She was horrified.

"It does sound like a hell of a coincidence, doesn't it?" he admitted.

"And Lonegan, impressed by your first spectacular success, asks you once again to solve a crime of the couch. Right?"

"I don't think I really want to get involved."

"Why not? You enjoyed tracking down the murderer of Jonathan Thomas."

"I had almost a need to find out who murdered Jonathan. He seemed so defenseless in life, and he certainly was after death. But I really don't care who murdered Mrs. Ga—er—this patient's husband."

"Darling, you don't have to hide the name. A front-page story in this afternoon's *Post* contained all the gory details of the murder of Albert Francis Garth, famous Wall Street broker. It took place in his elegant penthouse at some time between midnight and three this morning, according to the coroner. The murderer didn't leave a clue."

"You know more about it than I do," he muttered.

"You would have known too if you had time to read a newspaper or watch TV."

She was looking at him as though she wanted to say something.

"What is it?" he asked.

She smiled. "I offer my help, if you could use it."

"Like last time? You thought it was the butler." He laughed.

"The maid," she said defensively.

"Neither one of us should be involved, Mary."

"Wait a minute!" Her brown eyes widened. "Have

you considered that your patient might have murdered her husband?"

"Lonegan had the same thought."

"And you?"

"The first rule of analysis is that a patient tell the truth, no matter how embarrassing or shameful he believes it to be. Even if Mrs. Garth committed the murder and told me so, I could not reveal what she said in confidence to *anyone*. Not even the Supreme Court of the United States of America, backed by the army, navy, air force *and* marines."

"But patients don't always tell the truth."

"Not right away. It takes some a long time before they trust the analyst enough to tell the whole truth. Even on the couch preservation of the self comes first. Or what the patient believes to be preservation of the self. He doesn't know the greater self-preservation would be to face the truth as fast as possible."

"So that Mrs. Garth might have committed the murder in spite of the fact that she may tell you she is innocent."

Even Mary could envision Helene Garth as slayer of her husband. Dr. Ames told himself he had to be objective—that while he sympathized with the appealing, lost, helpless little girl trapped inside Helene Garth, this was no reason to rule out the possibility she might be capable of killing, for revenge or money, or both.

"I think I'll have a second drink before dinner," he announced.

He added, "And maybe a third."

SEVEN

The next afternoon at ten minutes to two he heard the outer door open and knew Helene Garth had arrived. He listened to the young lawyer who lay on the couch express some further thoughts about his father, and summed up the meaning of the young lawyer's associations that hour, before telling him he would see him the following day.

As Helene Garth walked into the room, Dr. Ames said, with a look of concern on his face, "I'm so sorry to hear of your husband's death."

"It was horrible." There were tears in her eyes.

"How do you feel?"

"I'm trying to pull myself together." She sat down, looking at him helplessly.

"Do you want to tell me what happened?" His voice was gentle. If she could talk about her feelings, rather than deny them, she would be better able to handle them.

"I feel I've talked my head off. The police questioned me for hours yesterday and today. They're trying to find clues to the murderer."

She was silent. He waited, his eyes on her, sympathetic, reassuring.

She said slowly, "I went to my bedroom early in the evening, undressed and watched television, waiting for Al to come home from a dinner meeting. He had not arrived by midnight, so I turned off the television and fell asleep. When I woke in the morning about eight, he wasn't in the bed. I was startled. It was the first time since we were married that I woke up alone in that apartment.

"I got out of bed and went into the living room. Then I saw him. He was stretched out on the floor on his back. His jacket and shirt were all bloody. The blood was all over the white carpet. At first I didn't believe what I saw. I thought I was having a nightmare, that I was still asleep. Then I screamed and ran out of the room.

"I ran through the dining room and kitchen to Vera's room, shouting 'Vera! Vera!' She came running out. I took her by the hand and led her to the living room. When she saw Al's body, she screamed too.

"I called the police, and they were there in ten minutes. They were pretty considerate, I must say, though later they asked a lot of questions. One detective kept after me as though he thought I killed Al."

"Could your husband have brought someone home while you were asleep without your hearing them enter the apartment?"

"Easily. I'm a sound sleeper. And the bedroom is at one end of a long hall. Also, Al had all the rooms soundproofed so he could read in his study while I watched television in the bedroom."

"Then you husband could have brought home a friend or stranger. They could have quarreled. Whoever it was could have killed him and slipped out of the apartment without you or the cook hearing him."

"Yes. The apartment has self-service elevators. And the doorman on the late shift goes down the street for a beer at certain times during the night, which all the tenants know. So a stranger could slip in or out of the building without anyone seeing him. The doorman told the detectives he did not see my husband come in, either alone or with anyone. Al must have arrived during one of the doorman's beer breaks. And if someone came home with Al, he could have left during another break."

"Did your husband ever mention a fight with anyone? Do you know of any possible enemies he might have on Wall Street?"

She laughed in spite of her grief. "You sound just like the detective." Then she answered, "No, he didn't mention fighting with anyone. I seem to have been his only enemy."

Dr. Ames felt he wanted a cigarette. He never smoked in the presence of patients and he knew that if he felt this nervous need some deeper thought was troubling him. Some half-conscious idea was coming up into his awareness but was being pushed back. He let his mind wander and the thought emerged. Perhaps, in spite of her denial and her look of innocence, Helene Garth's fury might have risen to the point of murder. Possibly, spurred on by some shred of self-preservation, either in panic or deliberately, she had killed the man who had

THE PSYCHIATRIST SAYS MURDER

attacked her. She was an actress — it was part of her profession to create a world of fantasy for the audience. Instinctively, though, he trusted her. He did not want to think that even to save her life she would be capable of killing. But he was not infallible. He could be wrong.

If she were telling the truth, she would be in desperate need of his help in facing the anguish caused by her husband's murder. It was not natural to turn the other cheek, as she too often had done, without some wish for revenge. And she would also sense another, even more profound loss. No matter how vicious her husband had been, his death would awaken the loss of an earlier tyrant in her life, but one who was beloved. Her father.

Dr. Ames asked in low tone, "Who do *you* think might have killed your husband?"

"I—I don't know."

"Not even the hint of suspicion? Did anyone you know hate him enough to kill him?"

"Several people hated him a lot. His first wife, for one. Marietta told me, one night when she came to the apartment to get an alimony payment Al's secretary had neglected to send, that she hated him more than she had ever hated another human being, including her alcoholic father."

"What about your relatives?"

Silence. Then, "I know my mother hated him. He once called her a stupid cow to her face. And she saw me with black eyes and bruises. She has often begged me to leave him. My brother hated Al too for his cruelty to me."

That added up to at least four who had hated Garth including her.

She was saying, "Why do I feel numb? I don't feel at all like crying. It's strange."

Not so strange, he thought. Her anger at her husband, even though she could never express it, was so strong it overpowered her grief. She also must feel great relief now to be free of daily threats and beatings.

Suddenly remembering he was curious as to what had stopped her from leaving, he asked, "Why did you stay at the apartment Monday night? You left here that afternoon confident you were going to get out for good."

She looked at him shamefaced and said, "When I reached the apartment, I fully intended to pack and leave before Al arrived from the office. I had just pulled my purple leather valise out of the closet when the phone rang. It was Al. He said he would not be home until late; that the partners were holding an emergency meeting. He never went into details about delays. He just said 'emergency meeting.' I don't know what made me do it but I said, 'You won't find me here. I'm leaving you.' I felt he couldn't stop me. I could leave before he got uptown. But instead of getting angry as I expected he would, he asked me—he sounded almost as if he were crying—to give him one more chance. He said, 'I need you, Helene.' He had never said that before. He also said, "Would you stay with me if I went into analysis?" He had never said that before either. What could I do? I stayed, waiting for him to come home. But then it got so late I fell asleep."

Thinking of another of her omissions, Dr. Ames asked, not in criticism but in concern, "Why didn't you tell me about Noel Marvin?"

She blushed. "I thought your opinion of me would be so low if I told you I had been having sex with another man while I was married that you would refuse to continue seeing me. Noel and I didn't see each other often. We didn't dare. But I needed Noel's love. Maybe the real reason I wanted to start analysis was that I wanted to get the courage to leave Al and marry Noel. It wasn't Al's money that kept me in the marriage. I don't think that much of money. I don't even need his money." Then sadly, she asked, "Why *couldn't* I break away?"

"You felt bound to him because in childhood you felt bound to a man like him."

"Noel Marvin is so different." She sounded as though she had to justify her choice of a second man. "He's kind and thoughtful. I met him when we played in *Leading Lady*. We had a brief affair. Then Al came on the scene and I was overwhelmed by him. He was so positive—Noel was much more casual about our relationship. Al insisted I marry him at once. Then he started being so cruel. Sometimes I would call Noel the next day and go to his apartment. Then I would feel enough of a woman to go home and face Al again."

"Does Noel Marvin know about your inheritance?"

"I tell him everything."

Not like your analyst, he thought. He said, "Then Noel Marvin might have killed your husband knowing you would inherit a large sum of money and might marry him."

"Jesus, no!" She gasped. "I don't think Noel could kill a fly. He's too sensitive. He's very moody and maybe he'll toss a barbed phrase now and then. But stab a man to death? No way."

"How do you feel about him now?"

"I don't know. I'm confused."

As well she might be. She would have to understand more of the reasons why she had chosen Garth as husband and Marvin as lover, before she could be happy with a man. There are men who hurt women, and men who protect woman, and she always chose men who hurt her.

"Oh, by the way," he said, "Lieutenant Lonegan, the detective in charge of the case, has asked me to help him. He wants me to interview everyone who is a suspect in the hope of turning up what he calls a psychological clue. I wanted to ask how you felt about this before I made the decision."

She stared at him, puzzled. Then she asked, "Do you want to help him?"

"How would you feel about it?"

"I think you should do all you can to help him. I want Al's murderer found. Or," hesitating, "do I?"

He looked at her with an intensity he hoped would

produce the truth, whether it be that she was innocent, guilty, knew who had killed her husband or unconsciously sensed who did.

She said slowly, "Dr. Ames, do you suspect I may have killed my husband?"

"I don't suspect you of anything, Mrs. Garth. Except perhaps of hiding a few facts. You didn't tell me about your affair with Noel Marvin though it is very important to you. There may be other facts you are concealing that I need to know in order to help you."

Tears came to her eyes. "I didn't kill Al," she said with conviction. "I thought of it, God knows. At times I despised him enough to wish him dead. But I couldn't kill anyone. I never gave up hope that somehow Al would change. That's why I stayed Monday night. I hoped we could make it. Part of me will always love Al for marrying me. For letting me be part of his life. For wanting me at least for a while. I will always be grateful to him. Kill him? Never."

"I believe you. And I want to help you live without the need to be hurt. I'd like to help you understand the reasons why you try to punish yourself."

"What can I do?"

"Try to become aware of some of the wishes and feelings you have denied over the years that have given you so much anxiety."

"What are they?"

"They will become known to you as the analysis goes on."

"Please tell me some of them."

It would be reassurance again, not analysis, if he explained. He knew she needed reassurance at this tragic moment. Perhaps he could help her by showing how her wishes and feelings appeared in disguised form in a dream. Too, it would be important for him to know what she dreamed after she learned of the murder. Her dreams would reveal the deeper thoughts and wishes that were being stirred into awareness by the tragic events of the night before.

Her dreams might even furnish a clue as to the murderer, or whomever she suspected. In dreams, he thought, we cannot deceive ourselves, as we do in daily, wide-awake life, about what we really feel.

He said, "Did you dream last night?"

"As a matter of fact," she said. "I had a terrifying dream."

"I thought you might have," he said. "Your day was full of such terror, it would have been odd if your feelings did not find some release by way of a dream. Tell me about it."

"Evan and I were running along a beach on a warm, sunny day. I stopped to pick up a beautiful shiny shell. I put it in a little pocket inside the bra of my bikini. Evan shouted 'Look!' He pointed to a black, slimy object that was rolling in on the tide. The waves pushed it higher and higher up the beach. I didn't want to look at it. It was obscene. But Evan kept insisting, 'Look, Helene, look!' It was a dead octopus with some of its tentacles cut off. A blackened, crippled monster. I screamed with fear. Then dark clouds blotted out the sun. Evan said,

'Let's bury it so nobody can see its obscene shape.' He dug a deep hole and we pushed the octopus-monster into the hole and covered it up."

She stopped, then said, "That was the dream."

He asked, "Did you and Evan often go to the beach when you were children?"

"As often as we could. We had a summer home in Westhampton and Evan and I would spend all our days on the beach." She laughed. "Of course, there are no octopuses in Westhampton. Only crabs."

"What does the octopus in your dream remind you of?"

"All those slimy tentacles, clutching at you, choking you to death." Her hand went involuntarily to her neck. "Al!"

"He tried to choke you Saturday night. Like an octopus."

"You mean in a dream an animal can stand for a person?"

"That's a very common displacement in the unconscious."

"Because I felt Al was like an octopus strangling me, I dream of him as an octopus. Fascinating!"

"Dreams use primitive symbols. The language of the dream is the language of the child and the savage. Let's see what else your dream is trying to tell you. What comes to mind about picking up a shiny shell and putting it in the bra of your bikini?"

"Evan and I would pick up pretty shells and carry them home."

"Would you carry them in your bathing suit?"

"We'd usually take along a large paper bag to hold shells. Oh! One day we forgot the bag and I carried home a very sharp shell in my hand. On the way it cut into my finger and it wouldn't stop bleeding. When my mother saw the blood, she screamed and took me to a doctor. He put three stitches in my finger. I still have the scar." She studied her left hand.

"And yesterday morning you saw blood all over your white carpet. Your husband's blood. Shed by a sharp object that cut into his chest. In the dream you and Evan bury the octopus-monster in the sand so no one will see its 'obscenity.' The dream seems to contain the wish that you and Evan had been able to get rid of your husband's body so no one would find it. The wish that Evan would come to your rescue once again, as he did in childhood when your father was mean to you."

"Why wouldn't I want anyone to find the body?"

"Because then you would escape feelings of guilt that come from an unconscious wish to kill your husband because he has tormented you. In the dream you picture your husband as dead, though no murderer appears. Which means his death reflects your wish. Evan helps you cover up the body and thus keeps you from being punished for your wish."

"I love Evan," she mused. "He has always understood my agony and protected me. I think he'd give his life for me."

Would he kill for her? Dr. Ames wondered. As Evan had once comforted his sister after their father's assault, would he do so as an adult, after her husband's attack? Comforting her did not necessarily mean he would commit murder for her, though.

"How would you feel if I interviewed your brother? And your mother? And Noel Marvin? As Lieutenant Lonegan has asked me to do?"

It would be a breach of classical psychoanalytic procedure. He never saw anyone but the patient. Yet this was a special situation. It was one that might involve the very life of his patient.

"Please see anyone you wish," she said. Then, "I have even been afraid that whoever killed Al might come after me next."

"Why?"

"Well, if it were Marietta, she might resent my inheriting most of his money. She might want to keep me from enjoying money that could have been hers."

"To whom do you leave it in your will?"

"I don't have a will. I never thought about Al dying. I guess I'll leave half to my mother and half to my brother."

"Talking about money, I am not going to charge you for his hour. I have used time that should be yours to try to settle in my own mind whether I want to help find your husband's murderer."

"Have you decided?"

"Not yet."

He added, "Aren't you afraid someone you love might prove to be the killer?"

She was silent.

"Shall I make a guess as to who it might be?" he asked.

She laughed nervously. "How could you know, at this point? You probably think it's my mother."

"It could be."

"Mother?" She was stunned. "But I was joking. Why do you suspect her?"

"Because of the powerful maternal instinct to protect the young from hurt."

Dubiously, she looked at him. "I can't see my mother as a murderer. She's never been able even to raise her voice in an argument."

"If she thought Albert Garth was wearing down your spirit and might even destroy your body in a drunken rage, she might be moved to kill him. How old is she?"

"Fifty-seven."

"She might believe that sacrificing what was left of her life was a small price to pay for saving yours."

"After you talk to my mother, you'll know she couldn't kill anyone." She paused, then, "I'd love to know what you think of her."

Love my mother, love me, he thought. He did not tell her that he had mentioned her mother because of the dream about an octopus-monster. Hiding the octopus also could have represented her wish to protect her mother from being discovered by the police.

He asked, "When is the funeral?"

"There isn't any. Al didn't want services or burial. He had instructed his lawyer that he be cremated."

The hour was up. He said, "I'll see you tomorrow."

She stopped in the doorway, said, "Whatever way you decide about taking on the case, thank you for wanting to help me, professionally and personally."

He still was not sure, in spite of her approval, that he wanted to get involved. But he would have to make up his mind in one hour. Lonegan said he would phone at four and he undoubtedly would. He was a detective who never gave up once he made up his mind.

EIGHT

Promptly at four, just after the patient who followed Helene Garth had left, his telephone rang. He had told the service he would take the call that came at that time.

He picked up the receiver. "Hello," not adding "Lonegan" in case it might be patient or colleague. He lit a cigarette.

"Hi, Doc. Right on time," said the deep voice. "Not to beat around the bush, did Mrs. Garth object to your helping me?"

"No, she didn't."

"Will you?"

He exhaled a puff of smoke. "I don't want to seem indecisive but I still haven't made up my mind."

"Tell you what, Doc, if I can set up all the interviews for one day, will you do it? That's all I ask. One lousy day. And if you come up with nothing, we'll call it quits. *And* I'll try to get the department to pay you for the day's work. You won't lose a cent. You figure up what it costs to cancel all your patients for that day and I'll make sure you're reimbursed."

Dr. Ames laughed. "You're determined to get me on the case, aren't you?"

"I think you're great, Doc. I also learn a lot from your methods. But, most important, I think you can really help solve this case."

"And if I fail?"

"At least we've both tried. Trying is better than not trying, when you know you should."

That did it. "Okay, Lonegan. I'll cancel all appointments for a week from today. I'll spend morning to midnight interviewing anyone you want. Don't worry about paying me. Consider it my contribution to New York's finest."

"I'll see you get some kind of reward."

"Forget that. You say you'll arrange the interviews?"

"With all the suspects. Except Mrs. Garth. You've already interviewed her, I gather, about the murder." There was sudden sharpness in Lonegan's voice.

"Yes. She says she didn't do it. I believe her."

"Go ahead and believe her. That's your privilege. But I have to think of everyone as a possible murderer. Nothing personal, you understand."

"Of course not. No more than you'd consider it personal if I turned up evidence against someone else."

The detective ignored the jibe. "I'll set up the interviews for next Wednesday. I'll phone you ahead of time and give you the names, the addresses and the hour of the interview."

"And I'll report to you after I've seen everyone."

"Call me at the house that night. Got the number?"

"Saved it from last year."

"I think you had a hunch, Doc, that we'd be working together again." Lonegan sounded amused.

"Maybe. But I didn't think it would hit so near home twice in a row." Dr. Ames winced.

"Just lucky, I guess." Hastily, he added, "I mean me."

Hearing the outer door open, Dr. Ames said, "Here's my next patient."

"Good luck, Doc. Hope you come up with a winner. I mean a loser."

"Thought you'd decided it was Mrs. Garth," he said sarcastically.

"No proof. But I'm digging away on that lady's alibi. Sure she didn't tell you anything I should know?"

"Only a dream, Lonegan. Are you interested in her dream the night after she learned of the murder?"

"Doc, when we convict a person on dreams, we're really in trouble."

"You can say that again, Lonegan. Such stuff as dreams are made of would hang us all on the spot."

And yet, he thought, after he hung up, there was something in her dream, if he could decipher it further, that might point to the murderer. That fragment of truth that was always at the core of a dream. An elusive fragment. Not enough, as yet, to make any sense.

NINE

"Well, I've done it," he announced to Mary as he walked into their apartment that evening.

He had the momentary fantasy that the portrait of his father hanging in the hall, an impressive painting of the rather stern man who had been a minor banking tycoon, smiled approvingly at him, which was more than his father had done when, at the age of twenty, Dr. Ames had announced, "I prefer to be a psychoanalyst rather than a banker." He was certain his father would have preferred him to be a detective rather than a psychoanalyst. His father could understand the reality of murder but not the terrors of the unconscious.

"Done what, Bill?" asked Mary.

"Don't you remember what I've had so much difficulty making up my mind to do?"

"Oh. You mean you've decided to help Lonegan again."

"You *did* know."

"You can't live with a man twenty years without knowing *some* important things about him."

"This isn't important. I'm giving Lonegan one day out of my life."

"A lot can happen in a day." She added, "Especially if it's a day of yours. Lonegan knows that."

Over the first scotch, he asked, "What's good on television?"

"What?" She was startled. "You never watch television."

"I thought there might be a good murder mystery." He tried to sound casual. "Maybe a Columbo episode. Or Banyon."

"Why, William, I didn't think you cared!"

She laughed in delight. She would often remain glued to the set for hours, mesmerized by murder after murder, while he worked in his study on notes for the next session of the class he taught at the Institute, or wrote a paper for a professional journal.

"You never can tell what you may learn on television about how to track down a murderer," he said.

"You're in luck," she said, scanning the Wednesday night television programs in *TV Guide*. "George Peppard plays Banecek. At eight-thirty."

"Is he a good detective?"

"Is he a good detective?" she repeated in mock horror. "He's unbelievably brillant. And appealing. And handsome."

"Give me time," he said. "I'll be right up there with Banacek and Columbo. With a friend like Lieutenant Lonegan and a wife like you, I don't need patients. I only need corpses."

TEN

The next day at noon, between patients, he called Lonegan who, his service reported, had phoned at eleven.

"Got a pen handy, Doc?" said Lonegan.

"Fire away."

"Here's the lineup. Next Wednesday at 10—hope that's not too early—you interview Mrs. Annette Benson at her apartment at 2 Sutton Place. She's Mrs. Garth's mother. At noon you go a few blocks north to 381 East 63rd Street to talk to Evan Benson, her son, and Mrs. Garth's brother. At 2 PM you have to be down at 2 Fifth Avenue to interview Mrs. Marietta Garth, the murdered man's first wife. Her daughter Amy is coming down from Poughkeepsie during the day and I asked her to be at your office at 4. Figured you'd want to talk to her when she wasn't with her mother. The last appointment at 6 is Noel Marvin, at his apartment at 69 Horatio Street. I'm sorry you have to go to the Village twice but that's the only hour Marvin is free. These temperamental actors."

"Looks like a busy day."

"And Doc, I'd better tell you all that we've found out so far." Muttering, "Not that it's much to go on."

"I'm listening."

"The murderer—he or she—was either in the house or was admitted by, or entered with, the murdered man sometime between 11 PM and 2 AM. There was no fight because nothing in the room was smashed or broken or out of place. That's how we know it wasn't an intruder. At some point the murderer pulled out a knife and plunged it into the victim's chest three times. The murderer then slipped out, taking the knife and leaving no prints. Not one lousy clue. Even the scent of heavy perfume would have disappeared by the time the body was found."

"That makes it seem you suspect a woman."

"Hell hath—and all that, you know."

"Still think it's my patient?"

"Eighty percent of homicides are committed by a member of the family. Husband or wife. Mother or father. Daughter or son. And a grandmother or grandfather or two."

"But Garth also had an ex-wife, and a daughter, both of whom probably hated him. And there was another man in the picture. Mrs. Garth's friend."

"Tell me, Doc." The deep voice was earnest. "If your patient confessed to you on the couch that she committed the murder, would you tell me?"

"It's academic, dear detective," said Dr. Ames. "Why go into the ethics of the matter, since she has not confessed?"

"But *would* you tell me?" Lonegan persisted.

Dr. Ames sighed. "I don't know. If by any chance she

confessed, I would have to take into consideration the possibility her confession was based on fantasy, if there was no proof of her guilt. Many innocent people have confessed to crimes they didn't commit because of guilt over incestuous or murderous fantasies of childhood. Since nothing ever disappears from the unconscious, where merely having the wish is the same as performing the act, a person will carry guilt around all his life because of his death wishes. Unless, of course, he is able to become aware of them and realize they are of childhood origin and he need suffer no guilt."

"You still haven't answered my question." Doggedly, he demanded, "Yes or no?"

"According to the ethics of my profession, I can't reveal anything a patient has told me to anyone. A patient must be able to trust his analyst one hundred percent." He added emphatically, "No exceptions!"

"Then you would protect a murderer?"

"I would try to persuade the patient who has committed a murder to confess his crime. I would try to help him understand that the inner guilt he is bound to suffer would be far more destructive to him than any punishment from outside."

This time the sigh came from the other end of the wire. "I guess you're really on the side of the law. Even if a patient was guilty, you'd want justice done."

"Exactly what do you mean by 'justice,' Lonegan?"

"Hey! I can't spend the day in debate over the meaning of justice."

Dr. Ames retorted, "You asked me about ethics."

"You win, Doc. Say, don't you have a patient waiting in the wings?"

"As a matter of fact, I do."

He heard the outer door open, signaling that his noon patient had arrived. He said, "I'll call you Wednesday night after I've seen the last suspect. Will you be home or at precinct headquarters?"

He wanted to sound like a member of the squad. After all, if he was into the investigation of a murder, he wanted to be into it all the way, like a regular.

"I'll be home after seven."

"Goodbye, until Wednesday."

"Good luck."

"I'll need it," he muttered, then thought, that's a strange thing for a psychoanalyst to say.

He wondered what his next patient would think if he told her he would not be seeing her at the regular hour on Wednesday because he was going to try to catch a murderer. He would of course give no reason. Let her fantasy take her where it would. It might be expressed in hostility, imagining he was going to a funeral (which some patients would imagine in their rage and accompanying death wish, equating cancellation of a session with desertion) while others in erotic fantasy would imagine he was spending the day in bed enjoying sex with wife or mistress. Unfortunately, he thought, the former fantasy would be closer to the truth.

ELEVEN

The Sutton Place apartment in which Helene Garth's mother lived was spacious and sun-filled. From the corner of Mrs. Benson's living room, where he sat on a flowered chintz couch, he could see the East River, hear an occasional ship passing on its way out to sea. Trees covered the dead end of 57th Street, which was a neighborhood park.

Mrs. Benson looked like an older version of her daughter, her once-fragile features set in hardness, her once-slim body burdened with additional weight.

"When the detective telephoned and asked me to see you, I was so happy," she said. "I wanted to thank you for helping Helene."

She added wistfully, "I wish I weren't so old. I'd start analysis too." Then she added, "But I really don't think it would do me much good." Sadly she said, "I've lived my life. The younger people can benefit more from psychotherapy."

Excuses, excuses, he thought. People reeled off dozens of excuses to escape facing inner conflicts, content to go on suffering and complaining and masochistically believing that was all life offered.

"Tell me something about yourself, Mrs. Benson." He pulled out a cigarette.

"Oh my, you smoke!" She looked at him reproachfully. "And you a doctor."

"I've come to terms with my suicidal wishes." He smiled, and lit the cigarette.

"Would you like some coffee? I always drink five cups a morning."

"If you have it made, fine. Black, please."

She bustled away to the kitchen and he looked around the room. There were photographs of Helene as a solemn baby, as a waiflike girl in ballet costume, as a college graduate in a long black gown, as the striptease dancer in *Leading Lady*. There were also photographs of a young man with blond hair and an esthetic face vaguely resembling Helene's, who undoubtedly was her brother Evan.

Mrs. Benson returned with two dainty china cups on a silver tray. As she sipped her coffee, chalk-white with cream, she said, "I don't know why you'd want to know about my life. It isn't very interesting. I was born in Racine, Wisconsin. I came to New York when I was twenty-one, thinking I would find fame and fortune as an actress. But instead, to support myself I had to work as secretary in a large manufacturing plant. My boss was a young man just starting his career as an executive. We fell in love, got married, and had two children. When he died he was a fairly rich man, so none of us have had to worry about our next meal."

"Was he a good father?"

"As fathers go. Oh, he'd lose his temper when the children misbehaved. But someone had to teach them to toe the line. I'm not very good when it comes to discipline. With me they always got away with murder."

And did one of them, in later life, literally try to get away with murder? he wondered.

"Did your husband ever punish them physically? By striking them?"

She tightened her lips while she thought. "I really don't remember. I think once or twice he may have lost his temper at Helene. Evan was always a quiet little boy. But Helene was fiery and would talk back to her father. He didn't like that. Yes, I remember his slapping her around a few times."

"How did you feel when he did this?"

"Oh, I wanted to stop him. But he was a very powerful man and when he lost his temper, you didn't dare oppose him. But he soon would snap out of it. Then he'd cuddle and kiss the children to make up for his meanness."

And, thought Dr. Ames, the inconsistency of first the violence, then a show of love, would confuse a small child who would wonder, how can my father both hate me and love me? How can I ever be sure of his love when one minute he attacks me, and then cuddles and kisses me? It was no accident Helene had married a man like Al Garth.

The picture was slowly unfolding of her childhood, sometimes punished by her father but sometimes also cherished as his little darling, seduced and dangerously charmed by him, as the Pied Piper charmed the children of Hamelin. And wasn't the flute in that old story a most fitting symbol for the penis? Her mother had tried to love the two children but probably was too frightened of her own sexual and aggressive feelings to create that sense of freedom a child needed to become emotionally independent.

"Did your husband ever strike you, Mrs. Benson?" he asked.

She looked embarassed. "Once."

"When was that?"

"When I dared to speak up for Helene. I thought he was wrong."

"Tell me about it." He sipped the black coffee.

"When Helene was in college she fell in love with a very nice boy from Yale. They wanted to get married. I saw no reason why they shouldn't. I told her so in front of her father. He disagreed. I argued with him and he struck me across the face. He said I was a stupid woman who was bent on ruining Helene's life. He insisted she finish college before she even think of marriage."

"So he struck you in front of his son and daughter. Did you ever hit him back?"

"Heavens, no!" She looked frightened. "He might have killed me if I had so much as raised an arm."

"How did you feel about Al Garth's treatment of your daughter?"

"I thought he was a beast, in spite of his good looks and his money."

"Did you ever reproach him for his behavior?"

"No. I never saw him when he was drunk and mean. I only saw Helene's bruises when she came here crying after he beat her up. I wanted her to leave him. I told her many times that she didn't have to stay with him just because she married him."

"What did she say?"

"She insisted she had to give her marriage a try. She said anyone had to stay married at least two years to see if it would work."

"Do you think Garth's money was one reason she stayed?"

"Helene is not a poor girl. Her father left her a substantial trust fund. And she earned money on Broadway. No, I don't think it was the money. I think it was more than the money."

"Such as?"

"Why, love, Dr. Ames, of course." As though he, a psychoanalyst, should surely know this.

"Do you think it was love Helene felt for her husband?"

"What *would* you call it?" she asked, perplexed.

"Passion. A kind of adolescent love. I would not call it mature love — a feeling that must include respect and understanding. I think only a woman who herself was immature emotionally would, even for a moment, entertain the idea of marrying a man like Al Garth, let alone marry him."

"But Helene didn't really know him before she married him."

"She could have waited until she knew more about

him *before* she married him. Where were her protective psychic antennae?"

Mrs. Benson laughed nervously. "You're way over my head. You doctors of the mind are too complicated for me. I'm just a simple mother."

That she thought of a mother as "simple" meant she had not been a very protective or understanding mother. She did not rush to save her little girl from physical attack by her own husband and so the little girl grew up to believe it was natural to be struck by the man who loved you.

As far as Dr. Ames could tell, Mrs. Benson was not the slayer of her hated son-in-law even though he had suggested this possibility to her daughter. A mother who would not protect her little girl from a beating would not protect her grown daughter, even though she might verbally protest an assault on her. She would be too frightened, in her words, of being "killed" if she raised a finger.

He could predict her indignant "of course I didn't kill Al!" were he even to suggest that she might have murdered her son-in-law. He would spare both her and himself the indignity of such a moment.

He stood up, said, "Thank you for the coffee, Mrs. Benson. And your cooperation."

"Is that all, Dr. Ames?" She sounded disappointed.

"You've been very kind to give me this much time."

"Did I help in any way?"

"You helped me understand more about your daughter and for that both she and I thank you."

"I thank *you* for the pleasure of meeting you. I'm only sorry it was a murder that brought us together."

Her handshake was warm and firm. He liked her, even though he thought she had not been a very emotionally nourishing mother.

TWELVE

Evan Benson looked just like his photograph except that
he was taller than Dr. Ames expected, standing about
six feet. He seemed a gentle man, the outgrowth of the
"quiet little boy" hie mother had described.

"Come in, Dr. Ames." He led the way into his studio
apartment, a few blocks north of where his mother
lived. From the windows Dr. Ames could see the many
towering buildings of midtown Manhattan.

Dr. Ames felt he was in the midst of a blaze of fire
when he looked around the room, twice the size of the
average city apartment. Its walls were lined with paintings that portrayed scenes straight out of hell. Billowing
flames of red, orange and yellow leaped from the depths
of black caverns. Devils with pitchforks raked the naked
bodies of men and women into the fires as dead-white
angels stared in helpless agony from the topmost
corners. If these paintings came out of the soul of Evan
Benson, it was a tortured soul indeed for, if ever Dr.
Ames had seen it, this was murder on canvas.

"Yes, they're mine," Benson said, as though answer-
ing the unspoken query. "They bring out quite violent
reactions in most beholders. I think that's why I paint
them."

Dr. Ames made a mental note: This is a man who, while appearing gentle, says he likes to bring out violence in others.

"They're very original," he said of the paintings.

"I sell quite a few, believe it or not. And for high prices."

"I believe it."

He admired the concept and the brilliant colors though he would rather not live with these scenes, especially if he should ever have to face them in the throes of a hangover, he thought.

Benson said, "Want a drink before lunch? I asked the maid, who also doubles as housekeeper, to make us shrimp salad and coffee."

"That's very thoughtful of you to provide lunch. I usually don't drink before the cocktail hour. But today is an unusual day so I think I will have a scotch and water, please."

Mother, daughter and son shared a warmth and quiet charm that was disarming, he thought, but also a vulnerability that made him feel protective. Yet this was the man Helene Garth looked to as her protector. Dr. Ames thought of her dream. Her brother, whom she loved, had helped her bury the octopus-monster in the sand so no one would see its obscenity. If taken literally, that meant she wished her husband dead and her brother to help her get rid of the body. But the story of a dream could never be taken literally. It was subject to many distortions, condensations and displacements. Sometimes the dream held the directly opposite meaning of the surface story.

Benson handed a drink to Dr. Ames and said, "So you're my sister's shrink." He spoke with admiration, not scorn. "Shrinks look more like actors every day."

"I take it that's a compliment," said Dr. Ames. "Unless you're referring to Boris Karloff." One of Mary's favorite killers.

"More to Richard Burton or Peter O'Toole."

"Glad about that." Dr. Ames took his scotch to a yellow contour chair and sat down.

Benson, lowering his six feet into a green contour chair across from Dr. Ames, said slowly, "I suppose Helene tells you everything, doesn't she?"

Dr. Ames thought he detected a slight note of fear in Benson's voice. He said, "What do you mean by 'everything?' "

Benson looked upset. "I only meant like — well, what a bum I am."

"Your sister doesn't think you're a bum. She thinks you are a gifted artist. And a successful one. She also speaks of you as her only protector. She loves you very much."

"That's good to hear."

The boyish eyes, gray like his sister's, were full of gratitude. Then they widened in alarm. "Or maybe not so good to hear. Maybe you think that to protect her I murdered the madman she married."

"I have no idea, nor do the police, who killed Albert Garth."

"Helene told me you were interviewing all the suspects to try to find out which one killed him."

"The detective in charge of the case thought I might

find some clue by talking to all of you. But it may well be that none of you is guilty. That an outsider committed the murder. Someone who had a grudge against Mr. Garth because he gave him the wrong financial advice. Or even a mistress he kept secret."

"He couldn't handle one woman sexually, let alone try for two," Benson said contemptuously.

"Sometimes a man can be potent with one kind of woman, impotent with another."

"I found that out in my own marriage." Ruefully, he added, "It wasn't long before my wife didn't appeal to me sexually. So I went out and picked up call girls. When she found out, she divorced me. I felt relief. I had wanted my freedom for a long time. Here I was, potent with a dame I paid one hundred dollars to lay. But I couldn't get an erection with my wife who was for free."

"Not for free, Mr. Benson. She probably cost you a lot more than the call girls in terms of psychic conflict."

"True. And I'm not about to try marriage again until I've been psychoanalyzed. I want to get over my repetition compulsion. Isn't that what Freud called it?"

"Are you planning to go into analysis?"

"Someday. When I can get up the courage. Seems I always follow in Helene's footsteps. So one of these days I too will go to a shrink. I know you can't take me as a patient. Analysts won't accept two members from the same family because of sibling rivalry. But maybe you can suggest someone for me."

Benson, with a smattering of Freudian jargon, threw

technical terms around as he did paint on canvas. He had a large enough income so he could embark on psychoanalysis, an income that would permit him to spend all his time painting those fiery, violent scenes on the wall. Was he capable of inflicting violence on another man, if aroused, even though his sublimation seemed successful?

Though Dr. Ames had not asked Benson's mother the question, he decided to ask it of her son: "Do you have any idea who stabbed Mr. Garth?"

Without the flicker of an eye, he answered, "Since he was the most hated man I ever knew, I couldn't possibly tell you all the people who probably wanted to kill him."

"The *most* hated man you ever knew?" Dr. Ames could not resist.

"You mean that, according to Freud, my father would be the most hated man I ever knew?"

"My question was below the belt. You are not on the couch. I apologize. But your sister told me how you came to her defense when your father struck her as a child for stealing. That was a brave act for a little boy."

"I was pretty brave then. I guess I was trying to make up for my father's lack of bravery."

"Then you could never be capable of murder," said Dr. Ames. "Brave men don't need to kill."

Came the answer, "I am not only capable of it, I have committed it ten times."

"Oh?"

"In Vietnam. I did murder — or at least I consider it

murder — at least ten other human beings. On orders, of course, on orders. But murder nonetheless. Murder without batting an eye. I had to kill to stay alive, so I was told."

His voice was light and gay, as though it had all been fantasy. Now Dr. Ames understood in part why Benson painted such scenes of hell. He exploded on canvas, where it would hurt no one, all his feelings of fear and rage over the horror that had been Vietnam. An artist, forced to kill, would try to combat his grief and guilt by painting away the terror.

"The detective said you were painting the night of the murder." Dr. Ames knew his voice was questioning.

The answer was swift, emphatic. "I didn't leave this room."

He strode over to a stack of canvases, pulled out a half-finished scene of a wasteland with huge red cactuses bristling on it. He showed it almost defiantly to Dr. Ames, saying "I was working on this."

"It's very imaginative." Dr. Ames nooded approvingly.

Benson replaced the canvas in the stacks, returned to his seat. Then, his gentle, gray eyes looking into Dr. Ames's, he took a sip of scotch and said, "Don't you want to ask me right out if I killed that miserable bastard?"

Dr. Ames said quietly, "I don't think you'd tell me if you had. And I don't want you to lie. If you did murder him, and wanted to tell me to ease your guilt and let the innocent off the hook, that would be another matter."

The young man smiled. "I think it's time for shrimp

salad and coffee. Mother said she was seeing you early this morning so I gather you will visit the first Mrs. Garth this afternoon. In that case, you'll need all the nourishment you can get."

As Dr. Ames speared a shrimp, he thought how much he admired the way Benson had avoided either confessing or denying the murder of Garth. He had, in his own words, "murdered" at least ten other people. But that was in a war sanctioned by the government, not in personal vendetta. Society decreed there was a difference. With the sanction, murder became civilized. Where there was no sanction, it was uncivilized.

After finishing lunch, Dr. Ames stood up to leave. He said, "Thank you very much, Mr. Benson, for your hospitality. You have been extremely thoughtful."

He walked to the door, Benson beside him. Then, spontaneously, partly out of sympathy for this tortured young man, the beloved brother of his patient, and partly as a protective gesture, Dr. Ames put his hand on Benson's shoulder.

He felt Benson's muscles tense and stiffen. Benson backed away, a look of distress on his face.

Dr. Ames did not know what to say. He wondered if the young man's repugnance was due to the fact that he was his sister's psychoanalyst and any touch by him would be taboo because he would be unconsciously equated with the father of Benson's childhood Dr. Ames suddenly remembered Helene Garth's tale of the time her brother had been whipped by his father when caught in homosexual play with the boy next door.

Perhaps, thought Dr. Ames, my touch reminds him of that traumatic experience and, if so, no wonder he recoiled in such fear.

He thought it better to say nothing about Benson's reaction. He opened the door and as he walked out, he said casually, "When you want the name of a psychoanalyst, please call me."

The look on Benson's esthetic face was now one of agony, as though he did not know how to apologize for his strange fear. Dr. Ames felt as near tears as he had been at times in his own analysis. He wished he had not tried to reassure Benson through a friendly gesture. Evidently it was not a touch of reassurance to the young man but a tentative assault.

THIRTEEN

The taxi raced south along Franklin D. Roosevelt Drive, then westward on Fourteenth Street and down to 2 Fifth Avenue. Albert Garth's first wife lived in an apartment on the nineteenth floor.

No man could have picked two wives more opposite in appearance, he thought, staring at the woman who opened the door. She was tall and willowy, clad in a navy print pants suit. Her curly hair, drawn high on her head, was jet black. Her facial features were sharp.

Her look was one of mild annoyance. She said, "Come in, Dr. Ames. Though I must warn you I'm seeing you only because the detective threatened that I'd be tossed in the jug, or other refined words to that effect, if I refused. I am outraged beyond belief to think I'd be a suspect. I have no motive. It's ridiculous to think I'd murder a man who has been giving me generous alimony. I don't get one red cent under his stinking will. Though I guess I should be grateful the alimony continues even if he's dead."

Dr. Ames wondered why she had to defend herself so strongly at once. As she talked, she preceded him into a room overlooking the arch of Washington Square, a

half-halo encircling the statue of the father of the
United States. The room was decorated in black and
white. Its only color was the red, blue and yellow of a
large abstract à la Mondrian.

If it had been winter, he felt she would not even have
been gracious enough to ask him to take off his coat. He
was glad Benson had provided a drink, salad and coffee.
He would be lucky if Marietta Garth offered him a
match for his cigarette.

He was accustomed to hostility from patients. He
welcomed it as a sign they were losing fear of expressing
inner hatred that was not really hurled at him but at the
parent of childhood, a previously denied hatred that in
subtle, oblique ways had been destroying them. But
hostility in a social setting was as unpleasant for a
psychoanalyst as for anyone else.

Marietta Garth looked about forty-five and, judging
by her anger at him, a man who had done nothing to
hurt her, he could well imagine the fury that could be
aroused by a man who *had* hurt her. Violent scenes
must have been played out between her and the late
Albert Garth. Unlike Helene, this woman could fight
back with a vengeance, he thought.

She did not ask him to sit down but he did so
anyway. She sat stiffly upright on a chair facing him,
glaring as he lit a cigarette, as though defying him to get
information from her.

"Mrs. Garth, I am not here to accuse you of
anything," he assured her. "Nor to question you. That is
Lieutenant Lonegan's province. I am here to ask your

help in trying to find out who could have killed your ex-husband."

"I could have! Cheerfully," she said in a vindictive tone. "But I didn't. Nor did my daughter. Amy wasn't even in New York at the time. How stupid can a detective be? Imagine ordering her to miss classes and come to the city to be interviewed."

"It was Amy's father who was murdered. I should think she'd want to help all she could to find his murderer. She just might recall something that was a clue."

"Well, I don't want to help. I'm glad he's dead. You can't imagine what an insufferable, egocentric, selfish human being Albert Garth was."

"But that doesn't give anyone the right to kill him. Only to leave him, if you were a woman who happened to be married to him."

"You psychoanalysts all think that punishment comes from within. That a man suffers enough from his own psychotic behavior. But I don't believe it. Monsters like Albert F. Garth — 'F' for fucking, or rather non-fucking as far as I was concerned—deserve the same beating they give others. I'm not a bit sorry he was knifed to death. And I'm sure the current Mrs. Garth isn't either if she received the same kind of treatment in and out of bed that I did.

"You can't imagine the torture of lying next to a man night after night, wanting him desperately to touch you, to say one loving word, only to have him turn his back to you, rigid with hate. It makes you feel despicable. As though you were not a woman. And you hate him because he can't be a man."

A different look came into her eyes, a look of curiosity rather than of anger. "Do you think she did it?" she asked, obviously referring to Helene Garth.

"No one has been accused," he said.

"What do you expect to get from me? A confession?" she demanded.

"Only if you killed him."

"I told you and I told that stupid detective that I didn't," she said haughtily.

"Do you have any idea who might have?"

"As a taxpayer, I am paying that inept detective to find out. I'm not going to do his dirty work."

"But you might help if you knew anything about Mr. Garth's past that might lead to the murderer."

"If I knew who he — or she — was, I'd pin a medal on them!" Defiantly, she added, "I don't care if the killer goes scot free."

What could he get from her but further verbal vitriol, he wondered. And what kind of daughter would this angry mother produce? He knew that underneath the anger lay hurt. She must have been very hurt as a child, long before Garth came into her life.

"Do you want to tell me about your childhood, Mrs. Garth?"

"The hell I do!"

He was amused at her childish defiance, at how much she *was* telling him in tone of voice and choice of words.

He tried another tack. "Do you have a career?"

Silence, as though deciding whether to deign to

answer. Then, "I'm a dress designer. Not one of the tops but I do show occasionally in Fifth Avenue windows."

"That's an elegant outfit you're wearing." He hoped to flatter her out of some of her acidity.

"Thank you." A grudging note of graciousness.

Then, as curiosity continued to get the better of her hostility, she asked, "Do *you* have any idea who killed Albert?"

"I don't have." He lit another cigarette.

She took one of her own cigarettes from a gold box on the coffee table in front of her.

"I didn't know you smoked or I would have offered you one of mine," he said.

He stood up, took out his lighter, held it to the end of her cigarette. Her defensive brown eyes met his alert blue ones. The brown eyes softened.

She said, "Please don't think I'm a shrew, Dr. Ames. It's just that for so many years I put up with such aggravation, not to mention terror, because of Albert Garth that I haven't energy left for one ounce of sympathy over his death. Or to care who killed him."

He said, as he had to Helene Garth, "You chose this man as husband. Nobody forced you to marry him. He must have met some of your unconscious needs."

She returned to the glare. "I don't believe all that conscious and unconscious crap."

"That's your privilege, Mrs. Garth."

And that's why your life is so unhappy, he thought, that's why you chose a pathological man like Garth. His second wife has just enough of the instinct of self-preservation left to seek help. But you are more self-destructive so you will live out the rest of your life in angry complaint.

Could she have murdered her former husband? She was certainly one person Garth would have admitted to his apartment late at night if she had unexpectedly appeared.

He asked, "Have you ever visited the present Garth home?"

"I went there about six months ago to pick up an alimony check. Albert's secretary took a vacation and forgot to tell her substitute to send it."

"And that was the only time you set foot in the apartment?"

Her eyes narrowed to slits. "If you're insinuating that I went there the night of the murder and killed him, forget it! I know my alibi sounds phoney. I can't produce one witness who saw me walking around the Square. But I do have my own kind of integrity. I don't tell lies."

"Did you meet Helene Garth when you were at the apartment?"

"We had a superficial chat. I told her how I felt about Albert and said I hoped she'd be happier with him. I also told her how much I admired her in *Leading Lady.* She's very gifted. When I heard she had married Albert, I pitied her as much as I pitied myself. He was an unlivable-with man. It was like living with a child. Not only a child but a rotten, spoiled child who never for one moment allowed you to express a feeling of your own."

Such tyranny would provoke the wish to murder in anyone, Dr. Ames knew. Especially when alcohol gave the unconscious free expression.

"Do you drink much, Mrs. Garth?" he asked.

"Once a week to excess," she said defiantly.

He laughed, "That's an unusual kind of drinking."

"I don't touch a drop six nights a week. But on Saturday, whether I'm alone watching television, or at a party, I drink myself first into gaiety, then into a coma. That way I sleep late Sunday and the day doesn't take so long to get through. I hate Sundays. All the dress shops are closed. And on a day when everyone else is resting, I don't feel like designing. I just feel like dying." She added bitterly, "But somehow I always make it to Monday."

He felt sorry for her in spite of her unpleasant defenses. Some people were lovable in their defenses but others, like Marietta Garth, were unlovable, as unlovable as she accused her former husband of being.

Dr. Ames thought he really could not find out much more about her. He stood up to leave. She snapped, "Where are you meeting Amy?"

"At my office. I'm on my way there now."

"It's a waste of time. For both of you."

He ignored her remark, said, "Thank you for seeing me against your will."

"I want you to know you're the first psychoanalyst to step inside this apartment," she said.

He was hard put to know whether she said it with pride or regret.

FOURTEEN

It seemed strange to arrive at his office at three forty-five in the afternoon. He had the leisure of fifteen minutes before Amy Garth was scheduled to arrive. He called his service to find out if there had been messages.

"Please call Lieutenant Lonegan right away," said the service. "He's at home. He left his number. It's—"

"Never mind. I know it by heart," Dr. Ames said in sarcasm.

He dialed the number, heard Lonegan's "Hello," and said, "I'm reporting in. Three down. Two to go."

"Glad you reached me, Doc, before you saw Amy Garth. She's not there yet, is she?" Lonegan sounded concerned.

"No. I'm alone."

"I wanted to catch you before you saw her. The doorman called this morning and confessed that he saw Amy Garth and her father arguing violently in front of the apartment at ten-thirty the night he was killed."

"Why didn't he tell you before?"

"He was scared to stick his neck out. He didn't want to admit he was on his way to the corner bar. But he said he thought things over and decided he'd better tell the truth."

"Exactly what did he say?"

"Just as he was leaving his post at the front door to go down the block 'for a little sandwich and beer,' as he put it, he saw a taxi draw up. Garth and his daughter stepped out. They were arguing. He heard Garth tell his daughter, 'I'll see you in hell first.' She had a 'mad look' on her face, he says. He walked away quickly because he didn't want to embarrass them."

"Just because they were arguing doesn't mean she killed her father, does it?"

"She could have gone upstairs and stabbed him, Doc. Maybe with a scissors she could have had in her pocket. We checked her alibi and found out she was *not* in her dormitory the night her father was murdered, as she says she was. I don't rule out daughters, especially in these days of drugs."

"Is Amy Garth on drugs?"

"I don't know. I thought that's one thing you might find out."

"I'll ask her."

At that moment his office doorbell rang. He said, "I think she's here. I'll call you tonight, Lonegan, after I've seen Noel Marvin."

"I'll be waiting, Doc. Oh, try to find out where Amy Garth spent the night, will you?"

"Okay."

Dr. Ames hung up and walked out to his reception room. Amy Garth was standing there; he recognized a pale edition of her mother, though she lacked the sophisticated look and, he would guess, the biting words. He felt sorry, without knowing her, for any daughter of a Marietta and an Albert Garth.

"Please come in, Miss Garth."

He led her into his office. He said, "I'm sorry to take you away from college but Lieutenant Lonegan thought it important that I see you."

He noticed she was wearing high white boots, a navy-blue miniskirt and white sweater moulded to her small breasts. Her dark hair swung low to the middle of her back.

"Oh, wow!" she said, walking to the window and looking out at Central Park, a blanket of green after days of the warmth of May sun. She turned to him with a faint smile, added, "Far out!"

"Please sit here, Miss Garth." He patted the brown tweed chair.

"First time I've been in a shrink's office," she said confidentially.

He doubted whether she could have murdered her father; parricide was an act rare in young women unless they were psychotic. But she might know something about his death, or sense a guilt in someone else. He doubted too whether she possessed the undiluted hatred of Albert Garth that her mother did. Even though a sadistic father inspired murderous hatred in a daughter, she would be apt to conceal it from herself to keep what she thought of as his love.

"You must be very upset over your father's death," he said sympathetically. She would be the one person whose feelings ran deep. Hated or loved, or both, he was her father. She was his only child and, while he could abandon a wife or two, he was not likely to desert a daughter.

Tears came to her eyes. Dr. Ames had touched easily vulnerable emotions. She was suddenly the hurt, desolate little girl whose father had walked out on her mother and her and now was forever taken from her by his death. Even if she had killed him, her unconscious would think of his death as irreparable loss.

Dr. Ames handed her the box of Kleenex. She took several pieces, blew her nose, then apologized, "Sorry to make such a fool of myself."

"It's not foolish to cry over a father's death."

She undoubtedly needed to cry her heart out, he thought. She probably did not dare cry in front of a mother who so openly hated her father. She would feel that to earn her mother's love she also had to show hatred of her father.

"What kind of man was your father to you?" he said gently.

The tears welled up again but she managed to get words out. "He was never easy to live with. He had a ferocious temper. Mother and he always fought like cats and dogs. My father and I had our fights too. But he never really hurt me."

Except when he walked out on you, thought Dr. Ames, and that is the deepest hurt of all.

"Can you think of anyone, Miss Garth, who might feel angry enough at your father to want to kill him?"

She turned in the chair and looked out the window,

as though stalling for time. Then she whirled around to face him again.

"Not my mother," she said. "You met her, I know. She called me yesterday and said she was being interviewed by you today. She probably told you how much she hated my father. But I don't think my mother could kill anyone. She wouldn't know what to do with a knife." She added, as though she had to explain, "I read in the papers that my father was stabbed with a knife."

"They haven't found the weapon yet. They think the killer took it with him."

"I hope they find my father's murderer." Again a stream of tears. And the cry of the bereaved child, "I'll never see him again! Never!"

She broke down and sobbed as though she had lost her whole world. And for the first time that day, Dr. Ames was glad Lonegan had asked him to interview the suspects for, if nothing else, he at least offered this pathetic young lady the chance to release some of her grief for a father suddenly and savagely murdered.

When she had quieted down, she apologized, saying, with a nervous laugh, "I owe you a box of Kleenex."

"Not at all. I'm glad you had use for it."

She said with sudden eagerness, "I wish I could answer your question as to who I think killed my father. But I really don't know."

"If you had to make a guess, who would it be?"
Silence.
He said, "Frankly, I have no idea either."
Still silence.

"Helene Garth?" he ventured.

"I don't think she would kill my father. No. Not Helene," she said thoughtfully.

Then with great reluctance she said, "The only one I can think of who might have a reason is that young actor, Noel Marvin, Helene's friend. I met him once at the apartment. My father told me he knew Helene was—" she stopped and blushed. Then she said, "Daddy had never used that word before, but he said 'fucking' Noel Marvin. Daddy said he didn't care, that he had given up on the marriage. Noel seemed like, well, like a man who might kill if my father taunted him. Noel's very nervous and kind of explosive. Have you met him?"

"Not yet."

He was surprised to learn Albert Garth knew of his wife's involvement with Marvin and surprised too that a father would use the word "fuck" in front of a daughter. It was one thing to say it in front of peers but to a daughter it was unusually brutal and sexual.

She said, almost sadly, "I don't want to prejudice you against Noel. But see what you think."

"By the way," he tried to sound casual, though it was the one question he was asking in deliberation, "the doorman at your father's apartment told detectives that he heard you and your father arguing violently outside the apartment building at ten-thirty the night he was murdered. The detectives also checked your alibi and learned you did not sleep in your dormitory that night, as you said you did."

"Oh, wow." She looked distressed.

"Do you want to tell me what happened?"

She bit her lips. "The whole thing is so sad that I didn't want to tell anyone. But I guess you should know the facts."

"You stayed in New York then?"

"No. I went back to Poughkeepsie that night. I caught the 11:20 train. I only came to New York that afternoon because my father ordered me to. My mother had told him that I— that I—" She stopped.

"That you were taking drugs?" He was following Lonegan's instructions to ask about drugs, although it did not really seem a likely possibility to him.

"Gosh no!" She looked at him reproachfully. "I'm not *that* self-destructive. It's a man. I'm very much in love." Defiantly, "I'm living with him in his apartment, though officially I have a room at the dorm. Johnny is manager of a large supermarket in Poughkeepsie. We plan to get married in the fall. Mother told Daddy this and he sent for me. I met him in the lobby of the Waldorf, where he had a dinner meeting, at ten o'clock. We took a taxi to his apartment. On the way he threatened to cut off my allowance and take me out of college if I didn't stop seeing Johnny at once. I told him I couldn't do this. That we were very much in love and intended to get married."

"That explains what the doorman overheard—your father saying he'd see you in hell first."

"My father is—was—a very selfish, stubborn man. He meant what he said. He would have taken me out of college rather than let me marry Johnny. Even so, I wish he hadn't died." Her eyes filled with tears.

"What did you do after your father said he would see you in hell first?"

"I walked away from him. I didn't trust myself as to what I might say. And I was crying. I caught a taxi on the corner and went to Grand Central and waited for the 11:20. I was so upset I wanted to get back to Johnny as soon as possible. I could have spent the night at my mother's but I didn't want to. I was mad at her for telling my father about Johnny and me."

"Can you prove you took that train to Poughkeepsie?"

"You could call Johnny and find out what time I got to his apartment."

"He might lie for you," Dr. Ames said gently, thinking of how the detective might reason.

She thought for a moment, then her eyes lit up. "There was the conductor. He ought to remember me. There weren't many people on the train at that hour. I asked him to wake me up when we reached Poughkeepsie, if I fell asleep. And then there's the taxi driver in Poughkeepsie who drove me to Johnny's apartment. He might remember me."

That would be up to Lonegan to find out, Dr. Ames though, musing how times had changed since he went to college. He wondered if, in spite of the so-called sexual freedom, boys and girls today made any happier choices when they married.

He said, "You've been very helpful, Miss Garth, and I

thank you for traveling all the way from Poughkeepsie."
He added, "I hope we meet someday under more
pleasant circumstances."

"I do too, Dr. Ames." She stood up looking as if she
didn't really want to leave and put out her hand in
gratitude.

As the door closed behind the white boots and the
blue miniskirt, he thought, she is a very appealing young
lady and, according to her, I am about to meet the man
whom she thinks could have killed her father.

He was curious to see the last suspect of the day, to
find out what kind of man Helene Garth chose as
successor to her husband. He wondered if by any chance
Amy Garth had intuitively identified her father's
murderer, if out of the mouths of babes again came
truth. Or, was she lying and had she killed her father,
the man who not only had deserted her but now
threatened to separate her from a young man she
desperately loved, reawakening all the fury and heart-
break that must have arisen when he, her father, had
abandoned her? Many, many murders were committed
only because the one who was deserted preferred to
take the life of the one he loved rather than give him up
to somebody else.

FIFTEEN

The taxi dropped him on Horatio Street at the western edge of Greenwich Village. It was the first time he had visited that part of Manhattan with its rows of renovated brownstones and he now understood why Greenwich had Village attached to it. There was the feeling of a spot remote from the steel-and-glass skyscrapers that towered north and south of it.

As the actor opened the door of his apartment, Dr. Ames thought that he was taller than he looked onstage, and his face had deeper lines.

But the voice was the same as in memory—low and rich. "Dr. Ames, how very nice of you to come downtown. Helene has told me all about you. I don't need to tell you how much she feels you are helping her."

The apartment, on the ground floor, boasted a garden which to Dr. Ames looked very inviting after a day that had been extraordinarily peripatetic for him. Seeing his guest's wistful look at the garden, Marvin asked, "Would you like to sit out there and have cocktails?"

"Splendid." This was a pleasure he was seldom offered in New York. You had to go on vacation to

111

Martha's Vineyard or Montauk to sit in the sun and enjoy a few drinks.

"A martini?"

"Scotch and water, if you don't mind."

"Why don't you go ahead out and I'll join you with the drinks."

Dr. Ames walked through a darkened room filled with overstuffed sofas and chairs. He lowered himself into a lounge chair that faced the foliage of bushes and pygmy trees. What could be more pleasant than a scene like this to end a difficult day, he thought. Noel Marvin seemed quite civilized; he wondered why Amy Garth thought him capable of murder. Perhaps it was just her adolescent fantasy that pictured Marvin as the slayer of her father; perhaps Marvin unconsciously symbolized her masculine self, the self that wished to attack the hated father. As a man she could hate her father, as a woman she dared not.

The actor strode out bearing a silver tray that held a shaker filled with martinis, a bottle of scotch, a bucket of ice, a pitcher of water and two glasses, one tall, one short.

"Thought you'd like to pour your own," he said.

"That's thoughtful." Dr. Ames preferred to mix his own drinks unless Mary, who knew his taste, was on hand. He liked the first one strong, each successive one weaker.

"That diligent detective grilled me four hours," said Marvin, lighting a cigarette and sitting in the other lounge chair. "I must have been his chief suspect for the role of murderer. Natural, I suppose, since Helene and I are lovers."

He added, squinting at Dr. Ames through dark glasses, "I trust she told you about us. That I'm not betraying a patient's sacred confidences."

"She told me."

He did not add that the telling had been delayed, forced by the murder of her husband. Delayed perhaps because of fear that her psychoanalyst would think her a whore instead of a virtuous wife.

"You don't have to believe me, Dr. Ames, but I didn't kill Garth." The actor flicked an ash from his cigarette into a cluster of pink geraniums. "I wanted to, he was such a shit to Helene. But I didn't think it was up to me to rid the world of him." Then he added, "He was such a sick, destructive man. I think sooner or later he would have divorced her, don't you?"

"Either that or killed her one night in a drunken rage. Did you ever see her after one of his assaults?"

"She turned up here one night with both eyes blackened and her arms bruised." The actor clenched his fists.

"What was your reaction?"

"I was furious at him. I wanted Helene to leave him. But I didn't want to kill him. I don't think I could kill a man. Not even in war."

"How did you escape the draft?"

"Do you think because I'm an actor, that means I'm gay? It was ulcers. I've had a weak stomach since high school. God, I'd last one week on Army food."

"By the way, I saw you in *Leading Lady* and thought you were excellent," said Dr. Ames. "You played the part with humor and great control."

"Thank you." Marvin raised his martini high. "That's salve to a wounded ego."

"Why is your ego wounded?"

"Because that detective imagined I could be guilty of murder." For the first time, his eyes showed anger and for a moment Dr. Ames thought this man might be capable of killing.

"Someone else—I can't divulge the name—described you as explosive and dramatic."

"I should hope so!" he exclaimed. "I'd hate to see an actor who wasn't."

"What play are you rehearsing in now?"

"The new Hal Prince musical. I think it will be one of Hal's best. And that's saying a lot."

Dr. Ames looked up at the clouds colored with sunset red. He asked, "When did you and Helene Garth meet?"

"During the casting of *Leading Lady*. We quickly became good friends, as they say. I don't have to beat about the bush with you. We had great sex. Many times, I wanted to ask her to marry me, but why would she marry a poor, struggling actor? I guess I was afraid of being rejected."

Many people try to relate to each other through sex, thought Dr. Ames. But the important thing was to relate in other areas too.

Marvin was saying, "The next thing I knew, someone introduced her to Albert Garth, a rather old Prince Charming but with money enough to buy her a million silver slippers. God, all that money. If I'd been that loaded, I would have asked her to marry me in a minute. Anyway, after the traditional whirlwind courtship, they were married."

"Did she ask you to their apartment?"

"A few times for supper. Once I met his daughter, a pretty, pathetic little thing. Another time—" he stopped.

"Yes?"

"I *hope* it's okay to tell you this. One night, about three months after they were married, I ran into Garth at the home of a mutual friend who turned out to be one of Al's accounts. Al had made a killing for him in the market. This friend was giving a party to celebrate."

"Was Helene there?"

"No."

"Didn't that seem strange to you?"

"No. This was an all-male affair."

"Who is this mutual friend?"

"I'd rather not say. I don't think he ever saw much of Al, other than as his broker."

"Why can't you name him—is he guilty of income-tax evasion because of large capital gains? Are you afraid I'll inform the Internal Revenue Service?" Dr. Ames spoke jokingly but he was curious as to the reason the actor wished to conceal the name of this mutual friend.

"Not that, of course." Marvin hesitated, then he said, "Our mutual friend is gay."

"I thought as much when you mentioned an all-male party."

"I'm not gay. And I don't think Al Garth was. But some men at the party were, including the host."

This introduced another element into the murder. One that might or might not be important. From what Helene Garth and, most recently, Marietta Garth, had told Dr. Ames of Garth's sexual behavior, it would not surprise him to learn that Garth was bisexual and occasionally sought homosexual experiences. There were more men in New York than one might suspect who lived in two worlds. The world of respectability with wife and children, and the world of undercover sex where erotic excitement and release could be obtained at the hands or lips or anus of another man. Such men needed the reassurance of a second penis to express sexual desire. To touch or see the penisless creature—woman—threw them into such sexual panic that an erection was impossible. Only if one understood his fear could one try to help such a man give up his fixation at the psychic age of childhood in which he felt attracted to the same sex.

"Did you know for a fact that Al Garth was not homosexual?" Dr. Ames asked.

"Not for a fact. But there were no signs of it that night. Several of the men were openly kissing and hugging each other. But he didn't join in."

"What was he doing there?"

"Celebrating his great kill on the market for our host, I guess."

"And you?"

"Celebrating the good luck of our host. Why are you

so suspicious?" Casually, he added, "I have many friends who are gay. If you rule out homosexuals in the world of the theater, man, you rule out eighty percent."

Then he asked, "How about another scotch? It's not often I entertain one of the nation's most famous psychoanalysts in my soot-filled garden."

"You're lucky to have this patch of earth to yourself."

"Couldn't you have a plot the size of Madison Square Garden if you wanted?" A look of resentment in his eyes as he added, almost accusingly, "If I had a lot of money, I'd want to show it off."

Dr. Ames laughed. "Think of the platoon of gardeners you'd need to take care of that much space. Mary and I have a pint-sized terrace where every so often the wind sweeps off everything in sight, including geranium pots." He added, "Thanks for the offer of a second drink, but I think I've had enough. It's been a long day and you've been very generous with your time as well as your liquor."

"I was kind of nervous about talking to you at first. Was I of any help?"

"I think so."

Noel Marvin had helped perhaps more than he had intended. Helene Garth had mentioned nothing of her husband's possible homosexual proclivities nor had she shown awareness of any homosexual tendency in him. But then, like many, she was what Dr. Ames thought of as "emotionally illiterate," unaware of her own hidden feelings or those of others. It was interesting, too, that both Helene's husband and her lover had been friendly with the same gay crowd.

Actually, Garth might have been the sort of man who, horrified at the idea of personal sexual contact with another man, enjoyed vicariously, in fantasy, the thought of sex between two other males.

Or, just as some girls will flirt with men yet retreat from any act of sex, he might enjoy taunting younger men trapped in their own homosexual urges. Perhaps under intense need, pushed by liquor to the edge of what he thought was obscene desire, Garth could even give in to his homosexual passion. Without knowing the man except through the words of others, Dr. Ames would guess that as a boy Garth had been so repressed sexually he never dared touch what he believed to be the mutilated bodies of girls.

Dr. Ames walked down Horatio Street, for the moment relaxed by the drink and the cool moments in the garden. But after a few blocks he felt discouraged. He had seen the last suspect but had not unearthed the iota of a clue showing that any one of those nearest and dearest to Garth, in love and in hate, was the killer.

SIXTEEN

He and Mary sat down to a supper of fried chicken
dipped in egg, bread crumbs, and basted with cream
sherry—one of Carrie's specials. After the first bite,
which he allowed himself to enjoy, he said in self-
reproach, "Lonegan's lost out this time. I haven't one
clue as to who killed Albert Garth."

"So it wasn't the cook," Mary joked.

He stared at her.

"Anything wrong? My nose not powdered? My hair
not combed?" she teased.

He said slowly, "Why didn't Lonegan include the
cook on his list?"

"You mean you think the cook did it?" She was
jubilant.

"No. But I think the cook could know something
without knowing she knows. And that I should talk to
her. Even if Lonegan omitted her."

"Lonegan isn't the type who thinks butlers and cooks
ever do it," she said.

"Vera's bedroom isn't far from the living room. She
might have heard something important. The sound of a
voice. Or a body falling. Or a door closing."

"Are you going to see her?"

"I'm going to call her, right now." He stood up.

"Before the sherried chicken?"

"I'll enjoy the chicken more after the call."

He went to his study, looked up Helene Garth's number in the telephone book, dialed it.

A feminine voice answered, not Helene Garth's. He asked, "May I speak to Vera?"

"This is Vera." A puzzled tone.

"My name is Dr. Ames. I'm a psychoanalyst and Mrs. Garth is my patient. I'd like to see you for a few minutes tonight, if it's convenient."

"Does Mrs. Garth say it's all right?" she asked worriedly.

"I'm sure she won't mind. You can ask her if you wish. I'll be there in about an hour. Please tell Mrs. Garth, if she's home."

He returned to the dining room and announced, "I'll see Vera as soon as I've eaten the sherried chicken." He was starved, since his last bite of food had been the shrimp salad at noon in Evan Benson's studio, consumed in the midst of those fiery paintings.

Mary beamed. "I'm so proud I've been able to contribute one small suggestion, Dr. Holmes."

"There's a new pants suit in it for you, dear Watson, if your suggestion turns up a clue."

"My money's on Vera." She folded her hands in mock prayer.

"That she's the killer?"

"Killer or provider of clue. Either way I get the pants suit?"

"Either way."

"Right on, then, oh sleuth of the psyche."

"Can't wait to get me out of the house, eh?"

"Can't wait for the new pants suit. One I'll have earned by my own wits." Delight was on her pretty face.

He mused, "Your years of reading and watching mysteries on television may finally pay off, Mary."

SEVENTEEN

Helene Garth lived high up in the penthouse of one of the tallest Madison Avenue apartment houses in the upper '70s. As the elevator sped him swiftly upward, he felt for the moment like an astronaut rocketing to the moon.

He rang the bell. Helene Garth opened the door, a radiant smile on her piquant face, as though she were greeting Freud. She said, "What a pleasure to have you as a visitor, Dr. Ames." She was wearing a floor-length red chiffon hostess gown. He thought, she is a beautiful young woman. Audiences must like to look at her motionless onstage, as well as enjoying the sight of her body when she dances.

She led him into the living room where a picture window looked west to the far hills of Jersey, shrouded in the deep blue of night with stars sparkling in scattered patches. Sunsets must be glorious from this height, he thought, and vowed that if Mary and he ever moved, their apartment would have a view to the west.

"May I get you a drink?" she asked.

"Do you have a brandy?"

"Is B & B okay?"

"Fine."

She poured the brandy from a crystal decanter on a glass bar in one corner. He looked carefully around the room, and judged from its walls of books that a large alcove to the left had served as Garth's study.

"Do you want me to call Vera?" she asked.

"Perhaps you'd better. She may be upset by my wanting to see her."

"I'll send her in. She can let me know when you're finished. I'll be in the bedroom."

"Thank you, Mrs. Garth."

As he waited, he studied the scene of the crime. The room displayed a decorator's precise and painstaking taste. The furniture was all shades of green. A sectional couch of deep-green velvet stretched in front of the window, two rounded jade-green chairs on each side. Paintings by Picasso and Renoir hung on the walls which were white, as was the wall-to-wall carpet. He looked for stains, but the blood of Albert Garth had been carefully cleaned away.

A plump woman with white hair, a rounded face and a worried look walked into the room. She stared at him uncertainly.

He said, "Vera, I'm Dr. Ames. I'd like to ask you a few questions. Will you sit there?" He indicated one of the jade-green chairs.

"Sit?"

She looked shocked. She probably never had sat down in that room, it occurred to him.

He seated himself on one end of the velvet couch. She

perched gingerly on the edge of the chair, as though it were proper to vacuum it but not to occupy it.

"Vera, the night Mr. Garth was killed, what did you do from eight o'clock on?"

"Like always, sir, after washing the supper dishes and the pots and pans, I went into my room and got ready for bed. I'm always very tired after a day's work. I got undressed, brushed my teeth, washed my face. Then I turned out the light. I was asleep in five minutes. I sleep very soundly. If you don't learn to do that in New York, you don't sleep at all."

"You heard nothing during the night?"

"Not a sound. I'm sorry, sir. But I do sleep like the Blarney stone."

"You're very lucky."

He wasn't, he thought. His decision to act on Mary's words, spoken in jest, yielded another zero. He didn't envy Lonegan his job. Too many dead ends too quickly. People connected to a crime did not speak half as freely as those on the couch, even the frightened ones, though of course the aims of psychoanalysis and crime detection were far different.

He decided to try another approach. "What did you think of Mr. Garth?"

Her mouth fell open. It was probably the first time she had been asked her opinion of any employer, he thought.

"He was always nice to me, sir."

"He never raised his voice to you?"

"No, sir. As a matter of fact, except for serving him

coffee in the morning and dinner, when he was home at night, I never saw him."

"Did you like him?"

"I didn't not like him, sir. I had no reason to have any feeling about him."

"Have you been married, Vera?"

She looked wistful. "I was married eleven years. Timothy died three years ago of a stroke. He worked on the docks. I had to find a job because he didn't leave any money and we had no children. If we'd had a son, he might have helped me out."

"Did you ever see or hear Mr. and Mrs. Garth fight?"

Hesitation. Then she said, "Once in a while he'd raise his voice at her."

"Just his voice?"

"That's all I know about, sir."

"Did you ever see him strike her?"

"Oh no, sir! Well, I never *saw* anything."

"I was wondering what you might have seen or heard."

"I never saw him hit her, sir."

"Do you think Mrs. Garth might have killed him?"

She stared at Dr. Ames as though he had asked if Helene Garth might have driven the nails into Jesus. "Mercy, no sir! Not that little lady."

"Why couldn't she?"

"She hadn't the strength, sir. It would take a powerful person to put that kind of knife into Mr. Garth."

"What kind of knife, Vera?"

"The kind used to open letters, sir." Her pale-blue eyes looked straight into his, expressionless.

"Do you know of such a knife, Vera?"

"Well, sir, I always made sure to shine the silver letter-opener on Mr. Garth's desk in the study there every week," pointing to the alcove. "Mrs. Garth gave it to him for his birthday last November. It was very sharp. It was shaped funny at one end. Like one of them old-fashioned swords."

Perhaps she meant a scimitar, he thought, recalling that he had seen such silver letter-openers in the men's department at Bonwit Teller.

"Where is the letter-opener now, Vera?"

"I don't know, sir. It disappeared. I didn't see it anywhere when I cleaned the room after—after—"

The pale-blue eyes darted to a large space in front of the glass bar, and he guessed the body must have fallen there.

Lonegan was depressed because no weapon had been found. Dr. Ames' hunch had been right, the cook *had* unconsciously revealed a very important clue, the weapon that had killed Garth. The weapon the murderer had taken when he fled the apartment. If this were all Dr. Ames could contribute to the solution of the case, it would justify his having donated a day he had considered wasted up to this moment. Except for the slight catharsis he had afforded Amy Garth for her grief.

"Thank you very much, Vera," he said. "You've been a great help."

"I can go now?" Relief on the plain face.

"Yes. Will you tell Mrs. Garth we're through?"

"Yes, sir." She rushed away with the speed, he thought, with which she must have fled the room after seeing the bloody body of the murdered man.

He felt elated by the brandy and Vera's disclosure. Lonegan also had undoubtedly questioned her, but before she was aware of the disappearance of the silver letter-opener. She was probably too scared when she did find it missing to call the detective.

Helene Garth returned and asked, "Will you have another brandy, Dr. Ames?" a beatific smile still on her face.

"Yes, thank you. May I talk to you a few moments? If you're not busy?"

"I have all the time in the world. Noel may be dropping in but not until later. This is so different, seeing you here." She walked to the bar to refill his glass.

"Not like an analytic session, eh?" He laughed.

"That's a different situation, isn't it, Dr. Ames?" she said. "It's unique. You can't really compare it to anything else."

"Right." he said. Then, "I'll come to the point. Vera told me that the silver letter-opener you gave your husband on his last birthday had disappeared from the top of the desk in the study. Do you have any idea where it is?"

"No. I haven't seen it, Dr. Ames."

Her answer came quickly, blandly. He knew her voice and its rhythms, knew its sound of anger, of grief, of fear, as it reached him from the chair in his office. He sensed she was not telling the truth.

"Did you inform the detectives of its disappearance?"

"No." Defensively. "I didn't know it was gone until Vera told me. Then I thought one of the detectives might have taken it as evidence and not mentioned it to me."

"The letter-opener was not in the study when the police searched it."

"The day after the Murder I—I just didn't notice whether it was there or not. There was too much else on my mind." She lowered her eyes like a bad girl expecting to be punished.

"You should tell Lieutenant Lonegan right away that the letter-opener has vanished, Mrs. Garth."

He did not wish to sound as though he were issuing a command, something he would never do in analysis. But he did want to protect her. He knew she was Lonegan's prime suspect.

"Of course, Dr. Ames. I'll call him the first thing in the morning."

"Do you want me to tell Lonegan?" he asked. "I'm supposed to call him tonight." He remembered he had promised to report to the detective after he had seen Noel Marvin.

"Would you?" She sounded relieved. "I'd be grateful."

"I'll tell him."

He stood up to leave, said, "I'll see you tomorrow, then, at two."

He shook her hand goodbye, something he did not do

in the office, but then this was not an analytic session. He thought she looked both victorious and upset. As though she had solved a difficult problem that had simply opened the door to new, harder problems.

He walked out of her apartment building and down the darkened street to where his car was parked a block away. Suddenly he had the uneasy feeling he was being followed. From his days as a navy lieutenant in World War II, he had been trained to react to outer signs of danger as well as the inner ones his analytic training had awakened him to.

He stopped, looked back. He thought he saw a shadowy form slip into the doorway of a building as he turned. But there was no one in sight.

He was almost at his car and he realized, as he dug into his pocket for the keys, that his hand was trembling. Fine detective you are, he told himself, afraid of a shadow.

EIGHTEEN

"Did I earn the pants suit?"

Mary looked up from the thriller she was reading, *Shock Wave* by Dorothy Salisbury Davis.

"You earned the pants suit. In sequins, if you want."

He walked over to her, kissed her warmly.

"Wow!" She closed the book. "Only a kiss like that would make me stop reading a book like this."

Then, curious, "Bill, what did you find out that warrants a sequined pants suit? And such a kiss?"

"Come listen to a phone call and you'll hear."

He looked at his wrist watch, it was ten o'clock, not too late to call Lonegan, who was probably eager to know if he had found any clue in the day's interviews. He dialed the detective's home.

"Hello." Lonegan's deep voice sounded very much awake.

"I've been wondering where the hell you were, Doc. You said you'd report in."

"It took me longer than I expected. I added one name to your list.

"Oh?"

"I didn't find out anything from the interviews. Then at supper my wife happened to mention half in jest—"

He stopped, Mary was hissing, "Not in jest!"

He went on, "— the cook at the Garth home. Mary reads every murder story she can get her hands on, including those written at the turn of the century in which the butler or cook usually did it."

There was a sound like a snort from Lonegan.

"On a hunch of my own, I went over and saw Vera. She gave me information I thought you should know."

"Yeah?" Skeptical.

"She told me that a silver letter-opener, very sharp, shaped like a scimitar—she said, 'old-fashioned sword'— had disappeared from the top of Garth's desk in the study. That room is really part of the living room, as you know. I wondered if the letter-opener could be the murder weapon?"

"Why didn't the blasted maid tell me that? I questioned her for an hour." Lonegan sounded furious.

"Because she didn't discover it until you and the other two detectives left."

"Did you ask Mrs. Garth about it?"

"Yes, and she said the same thing. That *she* hadn't told you because she didn't know it was gone until Vera told her. Then she thought you might have taken it as possible evidence."

"This is damned important, Doc. I'm going over and search that apartment this second." Lonegan's voice was clipped.

"It's pretty late."

"It's never too late where murder has been done. I

don't want Mrs. Garth to have a chance to get rid of that letter-opener if she's hidden it someplace."

"You still think she did it, Lonegan?" Dr. Ames felt Lonegan was following a prejudiced, fruitless lead.

"It's what I've been telling you all along, Doc. You just can't believe that a patient of yours could commit murder."

"I don't think she could commit murder." Thoughtfully, "Though I'm human, which means I'm not infallible."

"Doc, infallible or fallible, you're great! Talk to you later. I've got to hurry."

"If you find anything, will you call me when you get home? I don't go to bed before midnight." He wanted to know if Helene Garth was further involved in the murder.

"I'll call if I'm back before midnight."

"Or a little after."

"But no later than one."

"Okay."

As he hung up, Mary, who had remained glued to his side, repeated reproachfully, "It wasn't in jest."

"If you say so, dear."

"You'll eat those words, William, if that cook's clue leads to the murderer."

He did not believe Helene Garth could murder her husband for money, as Lonegan thought. She would of course welcome the extra money. But, as Freud said, money is never really important because only those things matter seriously to an adult that he wished for as a child.

If Helene Garth proved to be the killer of her husband, it would, he admitted, be one of the great surprises of his life.

NINETEEN

He stayed up past midnight waiting for Lonegan's call. Mary had gone to bed earlier, having finished *Shock Wave* and saying she was going to write the first fan letter of her life to the author.

For some reason he felt like once again reading the Schreber case, which Freud had titled "Psycho-analytic Notes Upon an Autobiographical Account of a Case of Paranoia (Dementia Paranoides)." In it Freud clearly formulated his theory that paranoia was a defense against homosexual desire.

If a man felt homosexual yearnings that caused him panic, he became paranoiac and imagined the other man hated him. As Freud succinctly put it:

". . . It is a remarkable fact that the familiar principal forms of paranoia can all be represented as contradictions of the single proposition: '*I* (a man) *love him* (a man),' and indeed that they exhaust all the possible ways in which such contraditions could be formulated.

"The proposition 'I (a man) love him' is contradicted by:

"(a) Delusions of persecution; for it loudly asserts: 'I do not love him—I hate him.'

"This contradiction, which could be expressed in no other way in the unconscious, cannot, however, become conscious to a paranoiac in this form. The mechanism of symptom formation in paranoia requires that internal perceptions, or feelings, shall be replaced by external perceptions. Consequently the proposition 'I hate him' becomes transformed by *projection* into another one; '*He hates* (persecutes) *me*, which will justify me in hating him.' And thus the unconscious feeling, which is in fact the motive force, makes its appearance as though it were the consequence of an external perception:

" 'I do not *love* him—I *hate* him, because HE PERSECUTES ME.'

"Observation leaves room for no doubt that the persecutor is someone who was once loved."

At twenty minutes past midnight, as he was still reading the case, seventy-seven pages long, the phone rang.

He lifted the receiver. "Hello, Lonegan."

The deep voice. "Supposing it wasn't me, Doc?"

"It had to be you at this hour."

"I'm home. I wanted to let you know I caught her red-handed."

"What do you mean?" Dr. Ames felt as if he'd been hit on the head with a rock.

"I warned you every second counted. I got there just in time. They were preparing to dispose of the murder weapon."

"They?"

"Your patient and her boyfriend. I caught them in the act, as we say about murder as well as sex."

"What act? You'll have to spell it out, Lonegan. I'm not too sharp after midnight."

"The silver letter-opener was plenty sharp." He apologized, "That's a rotten joke. Blame *it* on the hour."

"You found the letter-opener?"

"With their expert help. I mean inexpert help. It sure is a nasty-looking weapon. Artistic, though. The head of a heavily maned horse curves around the end of the handle. I wonder why she gave it to her husband as a birthday present? You'll have to explain that one to me sometime."

"Are you sure it was the murder weapon? Were there fingerprints on it?"

"Are you kidding, Doc? By this time? It was wiped clean of prints. And blood. But I'll bet her dainty prints once were on it. Maybe his too. Otherwise, why were they planning to get rid of it?"

"How?"

"Like amateurs. Rank amateurs. You won't believe it, but here's what happened. I rang the bell and the cook let me in. I asked where Mrs. Garth was and she says, looking goggle-eyed, 'In the kitchen with Mr. Marvin. They just sent me out.'

"I ran to the kitchen and there the two of them were. He stood holding the letter-opener. They seemed to be talking over what to do with it. They stared at me as if I were a two-headed man from Mars. I walked over to him, said 'May I have that?' and politely took the letter-opener out of his hand.

"Then I said to him, 'What were you going to do with

this?' He said, kind of embarrassed, 'Throw it down there.' He pointed to a chute that drops garbage to the basement.

"I said, 'I'll have to arrest you for trying to conceal evidence and on a charge of murder.' She said to me, 'He has absolutely nothing to do with it. He was helping me out.' I said, 'Then I'll have to book *you* on the charge of murder, Mrs. Garth.' "

Dr. Ames felt queasy for the first time since he had performed autopsies in medical school. Helene Garth had not told him the whole truth, but that did not upset him. He knew it took a while before a patient would trust an analyst enough to say everything that came to mind and, understanding the strength of defenses, no analyst ever gave up because of them. What upset him was that she might be guilty after all, and this made him question his own intuition.

"Where is Mrs. Garth now?" he asked.

"She's in the precinct jail for the night. She'll be taken to court in the morning. And I bet she's out on bail by noon. She can meet any amount the judge sets."

Helene Garth could weather one night in a precinct jail, harrowing though it might be. She might almost masochistically welcome it, Dr. Ames thought. He hoped she would be released in time to appear for her regular two o'clock appointment. She would need his help.

"Thanks for calling, Lonegan," he said. "Better get some sleep."

"You still think she's innocent, Doc?"

"She may be shielding someone. Had you thought of that?"

"Then why won't she say so?"

"I don't know. I'll try to find out if she shows up for her session tomorrow."

"If she tells you anything, will you let me know?"

"Of course. I want to help you as much as I can. As well as my patient."

"You'll be the Houdini of Manhattan if you pull that one off, Doc. I think the lady's interests and mine are directly opposed."

"We'll see."

"Want to make a bet?"

"I would never bet for or against a patient."

"Tell you what. If she's innocent, I'll but you all you can drink. If he's guilty, you don't have to buy me even one drink."

"You're overlooking one thing."

"What's that?"

"If she's guilty, I'll need the drinks even more."

Lonegan said gruffly, "Okay. I'll buy either way."

TWENTY

As the young lawyer on the couch continued his latest tirade against a tyrannical father, Dr. Ames heard the outer door of the reception room open. It was 1:55 PM. Helene Garth was out on bail and had arrived.

After the lawyer left, Dr. Ames looked into the reception room. She was standing there as though unable to gather the energy to sit down. She wore a black linen sheath that fell to her ankles. There were deep circles under the gray eyes.

She sank down on the brown tweed chair as if she wished she could disappear into it forever. In a dulled voice she said, "You know what happened, don't you?"

"Lonegan phoned just after midnight and told me he had arrested you." His voice was sympathetic.

"I was released on $20,000 bail. It was quite an experience." She winced.

He said gravely, "I'm certain Lonegan has made a mistake."

"No." She shook her head sadly. "I lied to you. I killed my husband."

He looked at her intently, said not a word.

She started to sob, tears streaming down her cheeks.

She pulled Kleenex after Kleenex from the box on the teak table.

Finally she stopped crying. She spoke haltingly. "I—I killed Al in self-defense. He—he came home very drunk about midnight. He struck me viciously across the face. I fell on the sofa. He said I would never live to leave him. He would kill me first.

"I—I was scared to death. I ran into the study. I picked up the silver letter-opener I had given him for his birthday. I went back into the living room. I stabbed him again and again."

She stopped. Then, "That's how it happened."

Dr. Ames asked, "Did a powerful man like your husband let a frail, delicate woman like you stab him three times without putting up a fight?"

"He—he was so drunk he could hardly stand on his feet. Much less defend himself."

He did not believe her. Everything he knew about her, plus his own judgment, told him she had originally spoken the truth and was now trying to shield someone. Someone she loved. Someone she knew had murdered her husband. She felt guilty enough to confess to a murder she had not committed. But the guilt stemmed from the earlier days of her life when her father was the target of an unconscious hate that could not be released.

He asked gently, "Whom are you trying to protect, Mrs. Garth?"

The gray eyes looked directly into his. "No one. I *am* guilty."

"Of lying, perhaps. But not of murder."

The gray eyes widened. "You don't believe me?"

"No. Why don't you tell me the truth? For your own good."

He tried to sound firm, as though he would settle for nothing but the truth, as though her words carried an import far beyond the usual analytic session.

She was silent.

"Are you protecting your mother?"

She shook her head from side to side.

"Mr. Garth's first wife?"

"No." Emphatic.

"His daughter?"

In a low voice, "No. Not Amy."

"That leaves only two others, Mrs. Garth."

The murderer might also be one of two men—her brother or her lover. Helene Garth would be likely to martyr herself for either one. Somewhere in his impressions of the day before as he interviewed the two men, impressions collected by both the conscious and unconscious parts of his mind, must lie a clue as to which one was guilty. Each was highly temperamental, each might be provoked into a fury that could explode into murder.

She was adamant throughout the rest of the session in maintaining her guilt. But somehow that dream of hers haunted him. It had clearly indicated she had hidden something about which she felt guilty, just as in childhood she hid the shell in the bra of her bikini. He knew now that in reality she had hidden the murder weapon, an act that stirred memories of the afternoon she had hidden the shell.

The more passionately she insisted she was the killer, the more convinced he was that she was protecting someone. Through his mind flashed the image of the shadow he believed he had seen as he left her home the night before.

TWENTY-ONE

That night after dinner he told Mary he wanted to take a walk. He wanted to relax for a while in the cool of Central Park, stimulated perhaps by his short stay in Noel Marvin's garden apartment.

"Want company?" A reluctant tone in her voice told him she would rather stay home to watch television or read.

"No thanks. I won't be long. Just until I walk off Carrie's fudge cake."

Once on the sidewalk, he headed for the park, thinking that even though he saw enough of it from his office window, it was not the same as walking through it—taking in the scent of spring flowers, feeling the soft, yielding earth underfoot and looking up at a roof of greenery.

He strode into the park at Seventy-second Street, breathing with pleasure the evening air, cooled by the darkness. He walked a few paces, then once again, as the night before, suddenly he had the feeling someone was following him.

He whirled around quickly. Though darkness had taken over the park, a street light illuminated the nearby area and he thought he saw a figure slide behind a tree, but he wasn't sure. He was aware of what tricks the imagination could play at night.

He thought of turning back; he knew the high crime rate of the city. But he had never been held up before as he strolled in this supposedly safe part of the Park and he refused to let his fantasies turn him into a coward.

There was no one in sight and he realized he felt slight fear. His experience during wartime at sea was no preparation for the attack of a mugger.

Reluctantly he did turn back and started for the exit at Fifth Avenue. As he passed the large maple tree behind which he thought he saw a figure slip, he walked a bit faster, telling himself, "You really are captured by nightmare fantasy, old boy."

He was a few feet past the tree when it hit, something had struck him across the back of the head—a plank, the butt of a gun, an iron fist—and down he went, and as he sank he heard a scream. It could not have come out of his throat because it was the high-pitched scream of a woman.

He came to awareness seeing a policeman bent over him and a young woman standing beside him peering into his face. The policeman was saying to the woman, "I think he's okay. Your scream probably saved his life."

The young woman was saying, "I saw this man jump out from behind that tree and hit him," pointing to Dr. Ames' prostrate figure, "on the head with a gun. I screamed, hoping some cop was near." Sarcastically, she added, "For a change."

The policeman said, in an even tone, "We're often nearer than you think if you'd give us a break and let us know when you need help."

Dr. Ames lifted his head. It hurt but at least it was intact, he thought.

The policeman asked, "Do you think you can stand, sir?" and placed his hand under Dr. Ames' elbow to help him up.

Shakily, his head still one intense ache, Dr. Ames managed, with the policeman's aid, to stand up. Now that he could move, he felt a raging fury at the man who had attacked him from the rear, not giving him a chance for a fair fight.

"I'm sorry this happened, sir," said the policeman. "But no place in the Park is safe to walk after dark. We try to keep the Park free of muggers but it isn't always possible. I wouldn't walk in it again, if I were you, after sunset."

"It's my fault," said Dr. Ames. "I guess I was offering myself as bait. Though I've often walked here at this hour and nothing more violent attacked me than a mosquito."

The young woman asked anxiously, "Are you all right? Don't you think you ought to go to a hospital for a check-up?"

"Thanks to you, I don't think much damage was done—except to my ego." He touched a lump the size of a purple grape on the back of his head.

"Lucky for you she screamed and the mugger wasn't able to snatch your wallet," said the policeman.

"I'm very grateful to you," Dr. Ames said to the

young woman. "May I have your name?" The least he could do was to send her two dozen roses, he thought.

"That's okay," she said casually. "It's my good deed for the day."

"No, really," he protested. "I'd like to know who you are. You may have saved my life."

"Forget it." She laughed and sauntered away.

"Dames," said the policeman. "You can't tell what they'll do."

"Not only dames," said Dr. Ames sourly, thinking of his assailant.

As he walked home he wondered if robbery *had* been the motive for the assault. He was certain now that he had seen his attacker slip behind the tree, as if he did not want his identity known. A thief who was a stranger to him would have probably casually sauntered along, pretending to be an innocent passerby. Someone afraid of recognition, however, might hide behind a tree. And now he was convinced that the night before, as he had walked to his car from Helene Garth's apartment, he had been followed.

Why would anyone want to kill him? Someone who believed he might know too much? Could it be that the murderer believed that in her analytic sessions Helene Garth had revealed his identity and he was afraid Dr. Ames would go to the police? Someone who knew he could rely on Helene Garth to keep silent, but not on her analyst?

He felt a slight elation, in spite of the throbbing in his head, because he had received confirmation of his firm belief that Helene Garth was not the killer. But she probably knew who the killer was. And though the killer had trusted her up to now, because he had not murdered her, for her own good as well as Dr. Ames' protection, she had to tell him the truth. She could no longer shield the man she knew had killed her husband.

It had to be a man, he thought, for the woman who had screamed saw the figure of a man. And it was not likely that a woman would hit him on the head with the butt of a gun. Which meant the murderer was either Helene Garth's brother or her lover.

Noel Marvin had been caught trying to help Helene Garth get rid of the murder weapon. Dr. Ames decided to make another visit to the actor's home. He did not fear another attack. His anger, one of justified wrath, now drove him head-long toward the truth.

TWENTY-TWO

Mary was reading in the living room as he walked in. She looked up, sensed at once from the look on his face that something was wrong.

"What is it, Bill?" She closed the book.

"Just a little conk on the head. Nothing serious. I was careless enough to walk in the park after dark. A woman screamed when she saw a man hit me over the head with a gun. A policeman came running. I'm okay." He touched the bump, winced, thinking he would have to sleep on his side for a few nights.

"Oh, Bill!" She ran to him, threw her arms around him. "I should have gone with you."

He laughed. "When you become an expert in karate, you may protect me in the park after dark."

"Did the policeman have any idea who did it?"

"The man ran away before anyone could really see him."

"Promise me you won't go in the park again after dark."

He was silent. Then, "Mary, this may sound wild, but I don't think it was an ordinary mugger."

"Oh?"

"I think it was the murderer of Albert Garth."

She gasped. "Why would he want to kill you?"

"Because he assumes Helene Garth told me his identity and I might go to the police."

"Then you're really in danger, Bill."

"Only if I don't unmask the killer first. Which I'm going to try to do at once. I want to stay alive."

"What are you thinking of doing?" There was alarm in her voice.

"First, I'm going to pay a visit to Noel Marvin and ask that young man a few questions. Then, if he convinces me of his innocence, I'm going to Helene Garth and insist she tell me what she knows."

"Please let me go with you."

"No. I can handle this alone. I don't want you near any possible danger."

"But what if you're attacked again?"

"This time I won't be stupid enough to let my guard down."

He did not want to confess this to Mary but there was something about the idea of tracking down a murderer, a man who threatened his life, that excited him. A primitive sense of closing in on the kill aroused sensations in his blood and viscera that challenged him. He understood why some men were driven to danger, thrived on it, if they had not made peace within themselves.

"If I don't call you in an hour, Mary, will you phone Lonegan and tell him what's happened? I'll either be at

Noel Marvin's—he knows the address—or at Helene Garth's, and he knows that one too."

She looked worried but she knew enough to allow him to do what he thought best without protest.

He kissed her, said, "We navy veterans can take a lot of punishment. And we usually get our man."

"That's the Northwest Mounted Police."

"I can wear two hats, can't I?" he said, thinking that one hat would feel pretty uncomfortable at this moment.

TWENTY-THREE

He stood outside Noel Marvin's garden apartment and rang the bell. He thought perhaps that Garth, knowing of the affair between his wife and Marvin, had confronted Marvin and threatened a divorce naming Marvin as co-respondent, thus depriving Helene of either a settlement or alimony. Whereupon Marvin had killed him and Helene was now protecting him out of love and because she hated her husband.

Or perhaps Marvin might have been blackmailing Garth because of his homosexuality. Garth had refused to be blackmailed any longer, and threatened to expose both the blackmail scheme and the affair, whereupon Marvin killed him. These were wild guesses, he thought, but he was driven to wild guesses at this point to try to save his own life.

As he stood ringing the bell, there was no fear in him. He did not believe Marvin, if guilty, would try to kill him on the spot, thus signing his own death warrant, for Lonegan would know Dr. Ames had gone to the apartment in search of the killer.

Funny, he mused, when you are out after the truth, you are not afraid. This was a different kind of truth than the one sought on the couch, where you dealt with the mere wish to commit murder on the part of the patient, which was destructive enough because of the guilt and the need to punish the self. But there was nothing more destructive than actual murder, for it put an end to all hope for both victim and killer.

He realized he had been ringing the bell for several minutes. He had not wanted to phone to announce that he was coming, for if Marvin were guilty he might flee. But perhaps Marvin was with Helene Garth; that would be natural in view of their professed love for each other. And now Dr. Ames felt foolish that he had raced down to Greenwich Village. He thought, I should have gone directly to Helene Garth's apartment.

Unconsciously he gave the door knob a twirl. The door swung open. It was not locked.

He thought perhaps Marvin had left it open deliberately because he was sitting in the garden and could not hear the bell. So he walked in.

The lamps in the living room were lit but the room was empty. He walked toward the garden, then saw the body. It was lying on the floor, face down, in front of the picture window. Blood streamed from a bullet wound in the head. Noel Marvin's last role was one of a corpse in his own home.

Dr. Ames' first reaction was to get away at one so he would not be incriminated. Then he thought, I should call the police. But there was only one thing to do, out of his obligation to Helene Garth. He didn't want Lonegan to accuse her of this crime too.

He turned and walked out of the apartment. As he hailed a taxi, he thought, "Two murders and an attempted third, the attack on my life. But at last I know who the murderer is."

He did not think the killer, paranoid though he must be, would try to silence Helene Garth. He would know, however, in fifteen minutes.

TWENTY-FOUR

For the second night in a row he was ringing the bell at Helene Garth's apartment. Only this time with a sizable bruise on the back of his scalp.

She opened the door; she was wearing a sleek white jersey pants suit. They gray eyes were reddened, as if she had been crying for hours. For one moment he wondered, "Did she commit both murders? Have I been wrong all along? I told Lonegan I was not infallible—might this be the proof? Could the attack in the park have been made by a mugger?"

"This is urgent," he said. "May I come in?"

"Of course."

She led him into the living room, but this time did not offer a drink.

He sat on one of the jade-green chairs, she, facing him on the other.

He said, "This is a very unusual, a very tragic situation. You must be completely honest with me. It may save your life and mine."

She stared at him, a broken doll.

"The evening started with my being hit over the head with the butt of a gun. I think the attacker wanted to kill me because he suspects you told me he killed your husband. I thought it might be Noel Marvin so I went to his apartment to ask for the truth. I found him on the floor of his living room—dead. Shot through the head."

"Good God!" She tried to pretend surprise but it was no use. He sensed she already knew of the murder.

"You insist you are guilty of your husband's murder. But I don't think you can convince anyone that you killed Noel Marvin. And I think your life may be in danger, even though you believe it is not. As well as my own life. So I am asking you for the truth. You are no longer my patient. You are an accessory to the crime of murder. Or homicide, as the police say."

Her eyes filled with tears. She looked at him mutely.

He said, "I know who killed your husband. And Noel Marvin. Why do you insist on protecting him?"

A cry of despair, a wail almost like an infant's. "Because he murdered my husband to save me! And he had to murder Noel to save himself. I told Noel, when he tried to help me get rid of the letter-opener, who killed my husband. Noel said he was going to the police, that he wouldn't let me take the blame."

"In both instances, Mrs. Garth, the murderer killed only to save himself."

"No!" In anguish, she went on, "He knew how cruel my husband was. He was afraid my husband would kill me when he found out about Noel and me."

"I think your husband knew all about you and Mr. Marvin from the very beginning. That he even encouraged the affair."

"Encouraged it?" The gray eyes looked shocked.

"I think that was part of your husband's emotional illness. He was chiefly voyeur, not participant. He was too frightened to take part in sexual acts unless under special circumstances. Didn't that occur to you in view of his impotency after the first few weeks of your marriage?"

"I thought it was my fault. That I wasn't alluring or feminine enough. At least that's what he said."

"That was how he tried to escape knowledge of his impotence. By blaming you. He was terrified of his sexual feelings."

"And I was the scapegoat?"

"Not entirely. You got a morbid pleasure out of the relationship. Both in being beaten by your husband and in the illicit relationship with Noel Marvin."

Then he asked, "Do you want to tell me how your husband's murder took place?"

"I wish I knew. Oh, how I wish I knew!" A cry of distress.

"Tell me what you know."

She sighed, in weariness and in resignation. "I never really lied to you, Dr. Ames. Unless you call the sin of omission a lie. On the night of the murder, I *did* go to bed alone. I *did* turn off the light about midnight, thinking Al had not as yet come home. I *did* fall asleep. Suddenly I woke to the sound of someone softly calling my name.

"I sat up in alarm. I said 'Who is it?' Al usually turned on the light and made a lot of noise when he came in.

As if he wanted to wake me. To my surprise I heard the whisper, 'It's me, sis. I need your help.' My brother, who always came to my rescue when I needed him, was now asking me for help.

"I turned on the light by my bed. I was slightly dazed. The way you are when suddenly wakened during that first hour of deep sleep. I said, 'Evan, what are you doing here so late?' Then, as I saw him more clearly, I knew something dreadful had happened. His eyes—those beautiful, sad eyes—were full of fear. And he was holding something awful in his hand. It was all bloody. It was the silver letter-opener. Evan's hands were bloody too.

"'My God!' I said, 'What happened?'

"'I killed him, Helene,' Evan said. 'I killed the son-of-a-bitch. He didn't deserve to live. Help me get rid of this.' He held out the letter-opener.

"I took him into the bathroom and we washed the blood off the letter-opener and his hands. Then I hid the letter-opener in my bureau drawer under a pile of bras."

The thought flashed to Dr. Ames' mind: Just as in her dream she hid the shiny shell in a pocket of her bikini bra. The dream had combined elements of a current trauma with a trauma of the past. Both contained the reality of blood—the blood of her husband in the current scene and her own blood shed by the shell's sharp edge in her childhood memory.

She was saying, "Then Evan and I went to the living room. I saw Al's body crumpled up on the floor in front of the bar. His blood was soaking into the white rug. I felt sick to my stomach. And yet, I also felt as if my brother had avenged all the hurt and shame Al had inflicted on me.

"I took two half-filled glasses of scotch that were on the coffee table and washed them in the kitchen. I put them back on the shelf of the bar. I had to step over Al's body to do it." She grimaced.

"Then I noticed one of Evan's paintings lying against the couch. I said, 'What's that doing here?'

"'I brought it over,' he said. 'Al wanted to buy it.'

"'You mean he asked you to bring over a painting so late at night?' I said. I could hardly believe it.

"'He called about midnight,' Evan said. 'He told me he had just got home from a late meeting. He asked if I were busy. I said no. He said he had just read high praise of my work by Emily Genauer and thought it about time he owned a Benson. He suggested I come over for a drink and bring any painting I wished. He would buy it on the spot. He said he knew you would like anything I painted.'

"Evan picked up the painting, put it under his arm, kissed me lightly on the lips, as he always does, and started for the door. I told him to wait ten minutes. It was ten of two and the doorman usually goes for a beer every hour on the hour."

Dr. Ames asked, "Why do you think your brother killed your husband?"

"Al probably started to tear me down and to threaten

a dirty law suit because of Noel and Evan couldn't stand it. He ran into the study, grabbed the letter-opener and stabbed Al."

Dr. Ames said thoughtfully, "I don't think it was as simple as that."

"What do you mean?" She stared at him.

He realized it had been no accident two nights before when he had pulled out the Schreber case. He had not consciously intended to reread it but his unconscious, the part of the mind that never sleeps, had directed him to this first important study of homosexuality. Partly because of what Noel Marvin had said, partly because of something he had sensed in Evan Benson.

He did not answer Helene Garth's question. Instead he said, "Where can I find your brother?"

She stood up, said quietly, "I'll get him. He's in my bedroom. He came back here in a panic after he killed Noel. Poor Noel." Her eyes filled with tears. "He tried to be so noble. Why couldn't he let well enough alone?"

"Because he loved you in his way and didn't want you to suffer needlessly," said Dr. Ames.

He added, "Before you bring in your brother, Mrs. Garth, may I ask if you realize how emotionally ill he is?"

"I think so, Dr. Ames. After he told me about Noel, I knew Evan must be desperate. His experience in Vietnam was too much for him. He got used to killing."

"Learning to kill the innocent in the interests of warfare certainly doesn't help men control their powerful natural urge to kill," he said. "But your brother has killed the innocent in this country out of murderous impulses that stemmed from his childhood. He was in a rage as a baby, as a boy, and as an adolescent. He needs long-term psychiatric help—if he ever has the chance to get it."

"I'm going to try to help him get it," she said. She added wistfully, "I will have the money—thanks to Evan."

She left the room and Dr. Ames thought of the young man who had committed two murders and had assaulted him, a young man whose life was filled with violence—a violence he had tried unsuccessfully to sublimate in his paintings.

Almost at once Helene Garth returned, her brother following her. He was not the charming, cheerful young man Dr. Ames had met in the studio. Benson seemed to have dropped all masks, retreated into a world of blankness. Dr. Ames recognized the signs of withdrawal. As a turtle draws his vulnerable head into a protective shell when he senses an enemy is near, Evan Benson had drawn an invisible armor over all feeling.

Helene Garth threw her arms around her brother as though to hide him and said, "Evan! Evan! Don't worry. You'll be freed. I'll tell the judge how vicious Al was. How he beat me mercilessly. Tried to strangle me and throw me off the terrace."

She reached up and caressed her brother's golden hair—as she probably had done many times as a little girl, Dr. Ames thought—with a look of love in her eyes. Her brother shook his head as though trying to break through his detachment.

She said softly, "I know you killed my husband to protect me."

Her brother held her close. His eyes, now warmed by emotion, met Dr. Ames' eyes over his sister's head and he said to Dr. Ames, "You know I killed him for another reason, don't you?"

"Yes," said Dr. Ames.

"What do you mean, Evan?" Helene Garth stepped out of her brother's arms.

"Sis, I killed the bastard because he made a pass at me." His voice pleaded with her to understand.

Her left hand flew to her lips as though to stifle a scream.

"Let's all sit down," said Dr. Ames.

He motioned Benson to take one of the jade-green chairs, Helene Garth sank into the other, and Dr. Ames sat on the green couch. He said to Benson, "Your sister has told me some of the facts. How Garth called you late at night and asked you to bring over one of your paintings. Will you go on from there?"

Benson said, "I'll be as honest as I can. I'm just starting to realize what I have done. Both times it was like I suddenly went mad, as if someone outside of me was directing me what to do."

The deeply disturbed person always blames someone else, the mother of infancy; the evil, wicked, bad mother who tells him what to do and what not to do, thought Dr. Ames, for that is the era of life that he has never been able to leave, psychically speaking.

Benson was saying, "I arrived here about twelve-thirty with my painting, one I called *Fury Unchained*. I honestly thought Garth wanted to buy it because of Emily Genauer's praise.

"He poured me a drink and took one himself. He was already quite drunk. He studied the painting and said he'd pay $15,000 for it. I told him this was too high. I even offered it free. I said, 'Take it as a wedding gift. I never did give Helene and you a present.' But he wrote out a check for $15,000 and put it on the coffee table. We had another drink. Then he started to ask personal questions. Why did I get a divorce? Was my wife any good in bed? What did I do for sex? I thought he was interested in a brother-in-law kind of way.

"We had several more drinks. It got to be one-thirty. I stood up to go home. I intended to leave the painting and the check. He walked over to me and before I knew what he was doing, he started to fondle me. I was paralyzed. But I think what horrified me most was that I began to respond to his touch. I actually wanted him to keep on. I could feel myself getting an erection.

"At first I protested with words. I said, 'Stop it, Al! You've had too much to drink. You don't know what you're doing.'

"He said, 'I can't stop, Evan. You've been tempting me for months. You're such a beautiful boy. You look like Helene. You move like Helene. I've got to have you.' He kept on.

"I thought in fury, so that's what the $15,000 is for. Not for my painting. For me.

"Something exploded inside me. I pushed him away. I could see the desk in the alcove and the silver letter-opener gleaming on it. I ran to the desk, grabbed the letter-opener. Then I ran back to the living room. I plunged the letter-opener into his chest three times. He didn't even defend himself. It was as though he expected me to kill him for what he had done. He fell slowly to the floor. I knew he was dead. I had the sense to pick up the check and put it in my pocket. Then I ran into Helene's room."

He wiped a perspiring forehead. "That's about it."

Helene Garth was moaning, "Evan! Evan! How could you?"

He turned to her, said accusingly, "How could *I*? How could *he*? Didn't you know your husband swung both ways? Jesus! My sister's husband making a pass at me!"

"Do you think I would have stayed with him if I'd known?" Torture in her voice.

"Didn't it ever occur to you?" Dr. Ames asked her.

"No." She shook her head. "I may be naive but it didn't."

"Didn't Mr. Marvin ever tell you?"

"Tell me what, Dr. Ames?"

"That he knew your husband occasionally paid a visit to the homosexual community?"

"He never breathed a word to me about Al."

Helen turned to her brother and said, "Evan, we've got to get help for you. That's all that matters now."

"What shall I do?" Benson asked Dr. Ames, a helpless look in his eyes.

In spite of the fact that this man had attacked him, and had murdered two other men, Dr. Ames felt pity, knowing that only the deepest desperation drove him to such acts of violence. A child's anger is violent, cruel, and it is stirred by the slightest of threats. If love does not ease it, provide the control for rage, it can erupt in later years as murder or suicide, which is murder of the self.

Dr. Ames said, "Call Detective Lonegan at his home at once. I'll give you the number. Tell him the truth. Free your sister from the charge against her. There are extenuating circumstances in the murder of Garth. You acted in self-defense against a sexual attack. The murder of Noel Marvin is another matter."

Brother and sister stood up as if realizing further conversation was futile until they had confessed. Benson said, "Thank you, Dr. Ames. I feel I'm returning to the world of sanity."

"Tell me, did you really intend to kill me in the park?" Dr. Ames asked.

Benson blushed. "I don't know. Something inside ordered me to kill you because you knew I had murdered Garth and would tell the police."

"But I didn't know," Dr. Ames said.

"Helene never told you?" Benson looked at her in surprise.

"No," she said.

"But you're supposed to tell your analyst everything." Her brother's voice was accusing, as though she had been unfaithful to herself.

"I would never tell on you, Evan," she said. "I love you."

"Did Dr. Ames guess?"

"I guessed," Dr. Ames said. "It wasn't difficult after Noel Marvin was eliminated as a suspect."

Helene Garth turned to Dr. Ames, said, "I hope you'll forgive me for keeping back some of the truth."

"There is nothing to forgive."

Then, remembering his real role in her life, he said, "I'll see you tomorrow at the regular hour."

She had returned to her status as patient and she would most certainly need his help, now more than ever. Though, he thought, since he had become so involved in her personal life, he would have to refer her to a colleague for further treatment. He could no longer be the impersonal, objective figure a psychoanalyst must be in order to give the most effective help.

He wrote out Lonegan's home telephone number, handed it to Benson, said goodnight, and left brother and sister to settle their accounts with the law.

He welcomed the short walk to his apartment, he wanted to think over what had happened. At the very start, in a sense Benson had subtly told him he had committed the crime, with his taunt, "Aren't you going to ask me right out if I killed that miserable bastard?" Dr. Ames recalled Benson had also said, almost as Dr. Ames entered his studio, "I suppose my sister tells you everything," as though fearing she had reported his guilt.

He had made a mental note that, though outwardly gentle, Benson liked to provoke a violent reaction. Yet, if Garth had not been a member of the family, Benson might not have killed him, Dr. Ames thought, as another clue fell into place.

He remembered the shudder of terror when he, an older man and, as the psychoanalyst of Benson's sister, a substitute member of the family, the fantasy father, had casually put his arm on the young man's shoulder. In Benson's unconscious, Dr. Ames' touch would have represented the start of a sexual attack.

As Garth touched Benson, it too must have evoked a violent physical reaction as it awakened memories of the beating he once received from his father for "disgracing" the family by sexually touching and being touched by the boy next door.

To allow his penis to be touched by a man was taboo enough, but a man who was also a member of the "family" was the great taboo. The sexual advances made by Garth were as though Benson's father himself had tried to seduce him. As Freud said, "Observation leaves room for no doubt that the persecutor is someone who was once loved."

If Benson had given in to the older man, this meant certain death for succumbing to an incestuous wish. He had to kill before he was killed. And then he had to kill again to protect himself from exposure of the crime—more forbidden "exposure." If Marvin had fingered him as the killer, Benson would have had to reveal the homosexual encounter between Garth and himself. An encounter which probably was a replica of the childhood tragedy, and which to him, as an adult, would have been unbearable.

The tortured Benson did not know what he was sexually. His sexual life with his wife had been one of disaster. The seeking of call girls showed he felt sexually inadequate with women. This anguished young man had never enjoyed the pleasure of sex with someone he loved.

Dr. Ames remembered Benson's words, "Seems I always follow in Helene's footsteps." His sister had been Garth's sexual partner and Garth wanted him to follow in her footsteps sexually.

Dr. Ames now understood why Garth had called the younger man at that particular moment. His wife had just told him she was leaving for good. Abandoned, he sought solace by seeking sex with a replacement. He unconsciously chose someone as near to her, and as nearly like her, as possible. Her desertion would also cause him to regress sexually so that, with enough alcohol to free inhibitions, he could give in to his homosexual urges. The physical beatings he had to inflict on a woman were, of course, also indicative of his sexual problem.

And Helene Garth's dream the night after the murder became clearer. The crippled, slimy octopus-monster washed up on the beach symbolized her murdered husband as he lay bloody and dead on the white carpet (the sand). The shiny shell she hid in her bikini was the silvery murder weapon which she had carried in her hand after washing it and hid under the bras in her dresser drawer. It also represented the shell which, when she was a child, had cut her finger as she carried it home from the beach, causing such a deep wound that a doctor had to take three stitches (there were three stabs in her husband's chest). Her associations to the dream, as she talked of cutting herself with the shell, told of a need to punish herself, probably out of guilt over her incestuous feelings for her adored brother.

Though she had not murdered her husband, she felt as guilty as if she had because of her hatred for him. Her brother had unconsciously selected as weapon the gift she had bestowed on her husband (a hostile gift, as Lonegan had indicated) to carry out the bloody deed for her.

In her dream she and Evan had stood alone on a deserted beach as they so often had stood alone as children. And as they now stood, two against the world, he to be charged with murder, she an accessory after the fact.

He hoped an understanding judge would be lenient with both, taking into account the young man's terror at a sexual assault and the love of a sister for a brother who had always come to her rescue.

TWENTY-FIVE

The two men seated themselves in an empty booth in the rear of a bar on Third Avenue near the 19th Precinct headquarters.

"I said I'd buy—either way," said Lonegan. "What'll it be, Doc?"

"Have you forgotten so soon?" They had met for a few drinks after the Thomas murder case.

"Scotch, wasn't it?"

"Right. With water."

"Two scotches and water, doll," Lonegan called to a passing waitress.

"What kind of a sentence do you think Benson will get?" Dr. Ames asked.

"Depends on the judge. Whether he thinks, at least in the case of Albert Garth, the attempted rape of a man by a man is as criminal as a man trying to rape a woman."

"We'll have to hope for a knowledgeable judge."

"That reminds me of an old joke, Doc. One Irishman says to another, 'The only happy Irishman is an unborn Irishman.' The second one says, 'Yeah, but how many of them are there?"

"You don't have much faith in the judiciary?"

"My faith in the judiciary can be measured by the amount of scotch in this watered drink." Lonegan nodded at the glass the waitress set in front of him.

Then he said, "They may make me a captain for solving the two murders. It doesn't seem fair I take all the credit."

"Be my guest. You're welcome to the cash *and* the credit."

"Tell me, Doc, why were you so sure Mrs. Garth was innocent?"

"After years of treating people you can generally sense when they speak the truth."

"And tell me something else, Doc. Why does a beautiful dame like that marry a guy like Garth?"

"She thought she was in love."

"Wasn't she?"

"She was caught in the fantasy of love."

"What's a fantasy?" Apologetically, "I don't know beans about your profession." He added in a mutter, "Though you know plenty about mine."

"A fantasy is a distorted idea you've carried with you since childhood. A child sleeping in the same room with his mother and father sees them in the sexual act and has the fantasy his father is murdering his mother. He is too young to know about genital sex, but he knows about anger. So he interprets the act of sex as one of violence."

"You mean Mrs. Garth's idea of love wasn't love at all?"

"Right. It was a lot of other things."

"Like what?"

"Like masochism. Childhood sensuality. And hatred."

The detective seemed lost in thought. Then he said, "Something just struck me."

"What struck you, Lonegan?" Dr. Ames looked at the detective in amused affection.

"If Mrs. Garth had put that silver letter-opener back on the desk after she washed off the blood and her brother's prints, we might never have suspected it was the murder weapon."

"Right."

"Why didn't she?"

"I would guess she was in shock because her brother had killed her husband. And she wanted to protect her brother."

"So she made a blunder?"

"She was too upset to think straight. When we get upset, our unconscious thinking often takes over our logical thinking. If you'll pardon the jargon, at that moment Helene Garth was being controlled by unconscious guilt."

"Guilt over what, Doc?"

"Because she shared her brother's wish to kill her husband. Just as in earlier life she shared her brother's wish to kill their father, a cruel man, like Garth. And she unconsciously set it up so that she too would have to be judged for her guilt in the crime. For helping to conceal evidence and for protecting—I guess the legal word is 'harboring'—a criminal. She thought of her brother as the White Knight who would slay all the monsters who attacked her. He in turn was willing to play the part."

"Did she egg him on to the murder?"

"A good question. She probably built up her brother's hatred of her husband by telling him of the beatings. And by using his studio at times as a refuge when Garth attacked her, she kept going the undercover sexual attraction she had always felt for her brother, a natural attraction, one you find in every family, even though it may be denied."

Dr. Ames took a few sips of scotch. "It was a senseless violence, Lonegan. There was no need to murder. If Benson had not been afraid of his own powerful sexual urges, he would not have felt so threatened by temptation. He could have laughed off the sexual advance. Or reasoned with Garth. Or left the apartment. Garth was drunk and in all likelihood wouldn't have stopped him.

"Benson had choices. But his sexual torment, his fear of seduction, the memories of the beating his father gave him for daring to touch and be touched sexually by another boy, drove him to destroy Garth for the very desire he had to repress so intensely in himself.

"Benson was repelled by what to him was an obscene temptation. Too terrorized to reason, or to flee, his frenzy erupted in the violence he had learned to act out in Vietnam. Added to his slaughter of ten unknown victims on the battlefield was now the slaughter of a known victim. A man who had threatened him sexually and plunged him in memory to a time of childhood

178

horror. And then the slaughter of a second man, an innocent man, because he threatened to reveal the first slaughter."

Lonegan looked at Dr. Ames in mixed envy and admiration. "Sometimes I wish I'd set out to be a shrink," he said.

"It's not too late if you feel the urge."

"There's as much chance of that, Doc, as you turning in your diploma for a shield."

"No way!" Dr. Ames smiled. "I'll enjoy my sleuthing vicariously. Through you. And Mary."

"She helped on this one, didn't she?"

"I might not have interviewed the cook if Mary hadn't mentioned her." He added reflectively, "Mary and I often play into each other's interests without interfering."

"Isn't *that* love?"

"It's part of love. The sharing of other things besides sex. Wouldn't you say?"

"You're the super-shrink." Lonegan lifted his glass, "Here's to you, Doc."

Dr. Ames responded, "To you, Captain."

They sipped away in silence. Dr. Ames was the first to speak, He said slowly, "Let's also drink a toast to Helene Garth. She did help lead us to the killer."

Lonegan lifted his glass again. "What'll the toast be, Doc?"

"Let's hope that, after she knows herself better, she'll find a man whom she can really love."

"I'll drink to that," Lonegan said. He added reflectively, "Even if she was my best suspect."

Freeman
The psychiatrist says murder